Innocent Next Door

Shelley Munro

Munro Press

Innocent Next Door

Copyright © 2023 by Shelley Munro

Print ISBN: 978-1-99-106325-0
Large Print ISBN: 978-1-99-106353-3

Editor: Mary Moran

Cover: Kim Killion, The Killion Group, Inc.

Munro Press, New Zealand.

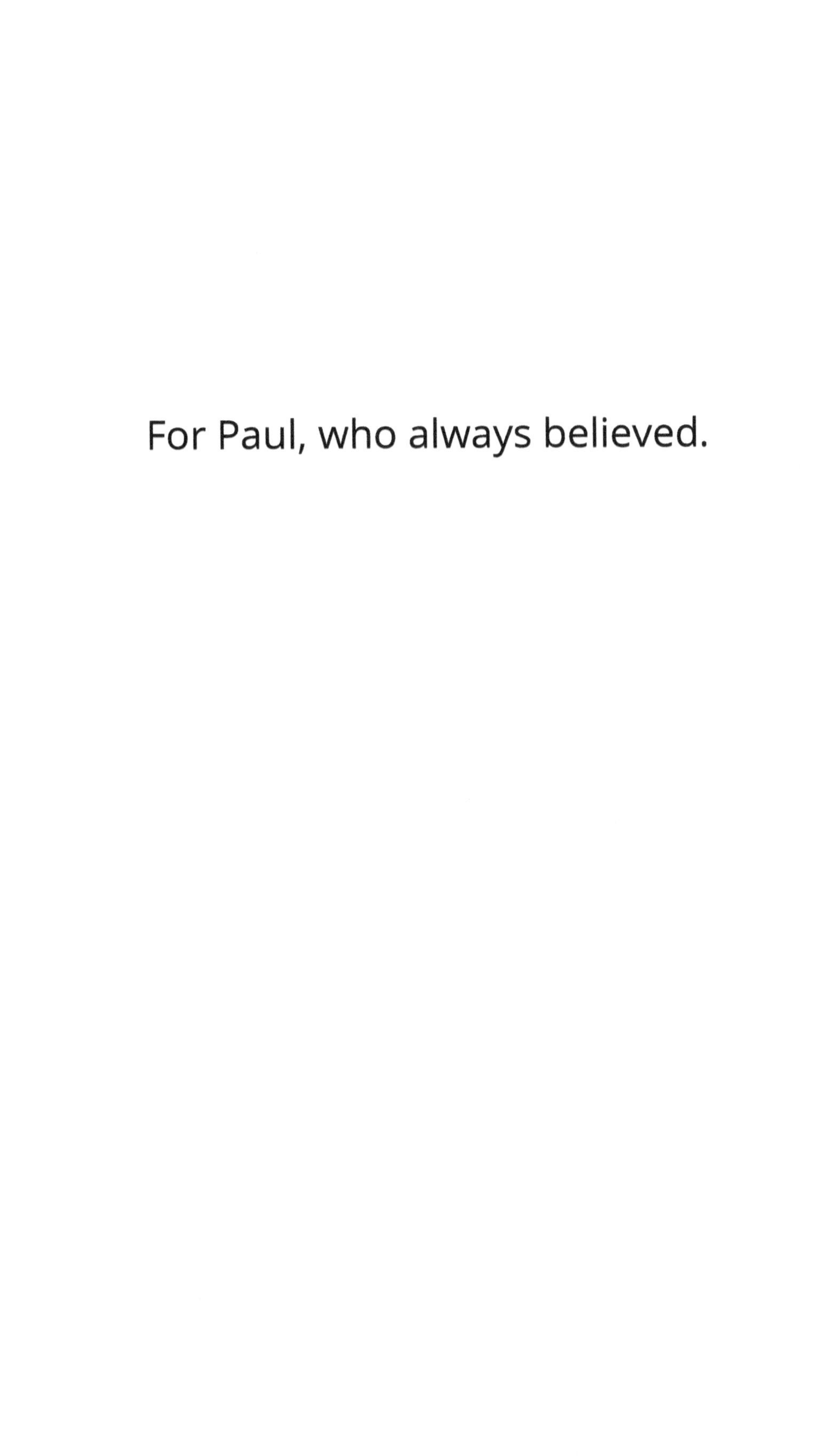

For Paul, who always believed.

Introduction

Adventure is Summer William's mission!

Life in a small town is comfortable, but living with her loving and overprotective family means it lacks adventure. And forget romance with two interfering army brothers around. It's time to leave the cozy nest. Her grandiose plans come to a grinding halt when she becomes innocently involved with a crime boss, then she bumps heads and lips with her uncle's sexy but very bossy neighbor.

Special Air Services soldier Nikolai Tarei owes his neighbor a favor, but looking out for his twenty-two-year-old niece is stretching friendship too far. She's a virgin, and her sex appeal, sassiness and brazen disregard for safety have Nikolai scrambling to protect both her and his battered heart.

Summer is a librarian who's a whiz at research. Now she's ready to try out the sex toys and sexual positions she's researched. The woman is tying Nikolai in sensual knots and driving him crazy—in and out of bed. But he's enjoying the journey, and suddenly he's thinking about making his Summer babysitting assignment a full-time commitment—if only he can persuade her to see things his way.

Chapter 1

"I'm not telling him. You tell him."

 "It was your fault. You left the book in the taxi," Marty snarled back at Ross. His hands curled to fists, and it looked as if he'd straighten the kink in his brother's nose with a hairsbreadth more provocation.

 Dare Martin had heard enough of their crap. He strode into his Auckland office and shut the door behind him. The soft thud of wood sliding home muted the chatter from the early dinner crowd in his restaurant and acted like a bomb explosion on his cousins. They whirled to face him, their familiar features bearing uneasiness and trepidation and a smidge of outright fear. He stepped away to halt his urge to grab their dumb-ass heads and bang them together.

"I hope you're fooling around." Dare growled, not bothering to hide his irritation, the reaction mild, considering the touchy subject. He dropped into the high-tech leather chair that sat behind the rimu-veneer desk and leaned back. They'd better be kidding, or he'd give them old-fashioned cement boots and drop them in the blue waters of the Hauraki Gulf. The book held an important place in his plans to take over the Ngataki family business, or a good portion of their trade. Their main competition when it came to profiting from drugs, the Ngataki men—especially Josiah—liked to mess with him and turn his life to chaos. Time for payback.

Hell, important be damned.

The book was bloody essential. Josiah had stolen his girlfriend—a woman he'd genuinely liked. He didn't intend to lose out to Josiah again.

"Where's the book?" His normal lazy drawl flattened to crisp and no-nonsense.

Marty backed up and edged to the door, his chubby face paling to reveal a mug full of freckles. "Ross left it in the cab. We realized we'd lost...ah...left it and grabbed another taxi to follow. When we caught up with the driver, he said there was nothing left on his backseat."

Ross nodded in emphasis, reminding Dare of a wooden puppet. "Yeah, it wasn't there."

Marty glared at his brother then continued. "We'd followed the vehicle and saw him drop off at the library on

Wellesley Street. A woman got out with a loada parcels. I think she thought our package belonged to her and took it with her."

Pissed yielded swiftly to fury, but apart from lifting his hands to grip the edge of the desk, Dare kept his expression impassive. "I want that book."

Marty scratched his head. "We couldn't find her in the library, but turns out the bird works there. We saw her leave and followed her home to Bottle Top Bay, boss."

"Yeah, young bird. Nice tits." Ross' brows waggled up and down, and he smirked the dopey grin that never failed to prod Dare's temper.

"If you know where she lives, then get the friggin' book back!" Dare roared, letting rip with his frustration. Goddamn bloody relatives. "I don't give a rat's arse how you do it. Just get it back."

"Sure, boss." Marty's beefy hand reached for the wooden doorknob. "The house is isolated—just the one next door. Breaking in won't be a problem." His words ran together, a sure sign he sensed how close they stepped to bodily harm.

"Yeah, no problem, boss," Ross said, stroking his bearded chin.

Dare sucked in a deep breath. A bloody farce, that was what this was. No wonder he'd discovered a gray hair this morning. After another calming inhalation, he flipped a red hardbound book open and reached for his engraved silver pen to add a notation to the margin. A soft shuffle of shoes made his head jerk up. "You still here?"

"Need a car," Ross muttered.

"Steal one." Dare seethed as he

delivered the obvious answer. The blow his cousin had copped during that brawl last year had left him two sandwiches short of a picnic. "And don't get caught because I won't bail you out."

Dare gripped his pen and concentrated on his coded notes. Lumbering footsteps followed by a click as the door shut indicated his cousins' departure. Dare tossed the pen down in disgust and leaned back. His chair slid smoothly into a reclining position.

He had a goal, a vision of power and his future.

Nothing would derail his dream.

Chapter 2

"I want you to look after Summer."

Summer's bare feet froze outside the door to her Uncle Henry's study. Her hand slid from the brass doorknob. A babysitter? Indignation stabbed her mind, robbing her of the sense of accomplishment she'd experienced seconds earlier.

At age twenty-two, why did they think she needed a babysitter? Her eyes narrowed as she placed her package on a wooden pedestal table and pressed closer to eavesdrop.

"Do I look like a babysitter?" a masculine voice snapped. "Try the yellow pages."

Summer nodded emphatically, giving a silent cheer for the owner of the low, husky voice. Way to go, mister. But while she waited for Uncle Henry's comeback, she fumed.

She knew exactly where the idea had originated—her family, or more specifically, her mother who thought danger lurked behind every corner in sinful Auckland City.

After weeks of discussion, her mother had reluctantly agreed to her departure on the stipulation that she stay with Henry, her mother's younger brother, while she attended her course.

"Think of it as a favor."

"No."

The blunt, uncompromising answer pushed a smile to the surface. She liked this man. And she agreed with him one hundred percent. Yes, she'd been a sickly child, but she'd outgrown the bad asthma attacks. As long as she used her preventer, there was nothing wrong with her health. She glanced down at her bust and hips, her expression turning rueful. Thanks to her mother's excellent cooking, her body—well, the polite word was "curvaceous".

"Nikolai." Uncle Henry gave a heartfelt groan—one designed to raise sympathy. "My sister will make my life miserable. She'll hunt me down on my honeymoon."

Summer suppressed a snort as she flipped the end of her French braid over her shoulder. Why did Uncle Henry think she'd come to Auckland? Although her mother meant well, she was overprotective when it came to the baby of the family. And now she was doing the smothering thing by remote control, all the way from Eketahuna.

If she allowed this, her bid for freedom would end before it started. It was time her family let her make her own mistakes, let her fix any stuff-ups by herself. Let her live.

When her boss at the Eketahuna Library had suggested further training in Auckland, the possibilities had made her breathless. Eager. At last, a chance to spread her fledgling wings. Despite her parents' protests, she'd seized the opportunity with both hands.

And she wasn't about to allow anyone to take away the experience.

"Tell someone who cares. With my track record, I'm the last person you should ask."

A shiver goose-stepped down her spine. That voice... His decisive tone did things to her. She considered easing the door open a little farther to check out the body that matched the sexy rumble. Meeting men was high on her to-do list. No time like the present.

"I hate to do this," Uncle Henry said, "but I'm a desperate man. You owe me. That time I saved you from the broad in—"

The heartfelt curse lifted Summer's brows toward her hairline. She hadn't heard her brothers use that oath before, and they spilled some original ones if they thought they were alone.

"All right, dammit. I'll check on her now and then, but if I see one girly tear, I'm outta there. And our debt is square once you get back."

"That should do it," Uncle Henry hastily agreed. "Just check to make sure her car is there and get a visual every couple of days."

Get a visual? Good grief. Nikolai was one of Uncle Henry's military friends. He'd take his duties seriously. This was not good.

"All I want is a peaceful honeymoon."

"All you want is to get laid," Nikolai muttered.

Uncle Henry chuckled—a smug masculine sound that made Summer ache to deck him on Veronica's behalf. "Yeah, that too."

Right, that did it. If she allowed this, she'd never escape her family's well-meaning influence. Yeah, she loved them, knew they loved her in return, but enough was enough.

Summer shoved the door open and strode through. "I'm back. Oh—" She stopped in front of her uncle's large wooden desk. Her hand fluttered to her left breast in pretend surprise while she studied her uncle's tan face. Handsome and burly, his recent happiness seemed dimmed by a hint of guilt or maybe that was her imagination. "You have a visitor."

"Summer, this is Nikolai Tarei. He's my closest neighbor."

Summer's gaze had already snapped to the man with the sexy voice. Physical awareness floored her, made her tongue stick to the roof of her mouth. Luckily, her brain continued to function and nothing impaired her twenty-twenty vision. Oh, boy. Tall, dark and sinfully sexy was welcome to guard her body any time.

Her uncle stood and rounded the desk to stand at her side. "Nikolai, my niece Summer. She's up in Auckland to do a six-month course at the Central Library."

Nikolai shoved away from the wall and

stepped across the faded blue carpet. "Pleased to meet you." He held out his hand in greeting.

Summer realized her mouth gaped and snapped it shut. She stuck out her hand, and instantly it was engulfed in his warm grasp. Her heart tap-danced, did a jig—the whole works. She fought the urge to jerk from the contact. One thing stood out in her mind. Miranda's Tips to Flirting could come in handy with him around.

He released her hand and stepped back. Summer's avid gaze followed as if attached by an umbilical cord. Big. Actually, make that huge. He towered over her by a good six inches. Broad shoulders gave his black T-shirt quite a workout. She took in his ruffled black hair, the stubble shading his jaw, his sensual mouth. Under no circumstances would she call him tame. Dark eyes that reminded her of the richest, most expensive chocolate skimmed her face, her body, then settled back on her uncle.

Stupidly, Summer felt the sting of rejection, but she told herself it didn't matter. Nikolai Tarei reminded her of her two brothers—extremely capable and overprotective. And one look told her it was likely he bore the bossy gene. She didn't require another brother-figure looking over her shoulder, vetting boyfriends, putting a dampener on her quest for independence. Not when she intended to let loose and live a little.

"I wanted you to meet Nikolai before I left. If you have any problems, you can call on him."

Uncle Henry's cheerful, gruff voice made her stiffen. Trying too hard. Did they think she was stupid?

"Most people would call that babysitting." She bared her teeth in a smile and intercepted the brief glance the two men exchanged—the quirk of brow, the silent grimace that said, "You deal with her".

Oh, for goodness sake. "I'm not expecting any problems. I'll be too busy." She paused a beat. "Going out on the town."

Uncle Henry spluttered. His mouth opened and closed several times.

"I have to go. I'm expecting a call," Nikolai said.

Summer choked back a laugh. In military terms that qualified as a strategic retreat. Wise man. She watched him saunter to the door and frowned. What should have been a loose-limbed stride had a distinct hitch, but his black jeans covered any evidence of an injury.

"Coward," Uncle Henry muttered.

Summer turned her gaze on her uncle. "Did you say something?"

"No."

Summer heard a distinct snicker and whipped her head around.

Nikolai's face displayed polite farewell. "Henry, see you when you get back. Give my love to Veronica."

"Right." The two men shook hands. "Thanks."

The silent communication thing again. She watched Nikolai exit and limp down the passage. Appreciation bloomed along with a grin at his mighty fine rear end. He might be her babysitter, her jailer, but she still appreciated the view.

She turned to her uncle. "What's wrong with Nikolai's leg?"

"Knee injury."

"On active duty?"

"Yeah."

Suspicion made her narrow her eyes. "Do Dillon and Josh know him?"

"Your brothers? Maybe."

A tight sensation gripped her chest. "Don't tell me he's Special Air Service."

"Okay." Uncle Henry blinked, his steady blue gaze not fooling her one bit. "I won't."

Nikolai limped down the uneven front path, heading for the gate in the boundary fence between his and Henry's property. He would've stomped if not for his blasted knee.

A babysitter.

Hell, he didn't need that sort of responsibility.

His foot skidded on a pile of damp grass clippings. Pain, sharp and jagged, lanced from his knee up his thigh. Nikolai glared at the green hose that spurted water into Henry's rose garden. He sucked in a pained breath, cursed and staggered to the gate, leaning his weight against it while he rode out the discomfort.

Babysitting. Hell, Henry should know better. Incapacitated the way he was now, he was about as useful as a gun without bullets.

Nikolai tested a little weight on his knee and decided he could make his kitchen without keeling over. The gate creaked open. He should have taken that damn painkiller before he went to Henry's. At least then, he might have an excuse for agreeing to Henry's blackmail. But no, he'd been drug-free, clear of mind and in total control, yet he'd still managed to find himself looking after a green country girl just out of high school.

He gritted his teeth as he hobbled the last few steps to his front door. Nikolai shouldered it open and headed straight for the kitchen and the bottle of pills. Five minutes later, he dropped into his recliner chair and stared out at his overgrown garden, past the knee-high grass and the scraggy shrubs.

He watched Henry carry a suitcase from the house and toss it into the rear of the car. Summer followed with a smaller bag and a suit in a protective cover. Nikolai saw her say something, heard Henry's booming laugh through the open window. His throat constricted with a feeling he hated to analyze as Henry swept his niece into a bone-crushing hug.

Hard to believe his friend and

mentor was married after years of the single life. Nikolai snorted. That was the kicker. Henry had sworn to remain a bachelor then taken one look at Veronica and fallen hard. They'd married quietly yesterday and were off on a cruise this evening, leaving from Veronica's apartment in the city. Hopefully, marriage would work for Henry. It sure as hell hadn't for him.

Nikolai thrust aside bitter memories to study Summer. Average height, long brown hair in a plait, on the chubby side, and a dazzling smile that made a man look twice despite the god-awful gray sack thing she was wearing.

His charge until Henry returned. Nikolai leaned back in the chair and closed his eyes. Hopefully, once a week would work. It couldn't be that bad.

A noise woke Summer. One moment she was dreaming of playing rugby with the All Blacks and the next her eyes sprang open, the fine hairs on her arms prickling in silent alarm. She froze, exhaling in a measured manner, while she listened.

There it was again—a muted creak. A footstep? She slid from bed, knowing she'd have to investigate or risk lying awake all night.

Whispers carried down the passage outside her room. A light flashed briefly and shut off.

"Must be in one of the bedrooms."

The guttural whisper snapped her to action. She crept to the window. The shutter clicked as she lifted the latch—loud enough for her to freeze in place.

"I'll check this room and the bathroom. You take the other two rooms."

"What about the girl?"

"You heard the boss. Do whatever's necessary to get the goods."

"Right."

Two of them. Healthy fear had her springing to action. She shoved the window open wide, no longer caring about attracting attention. Footsteps sounded outside her bedroom. The door handle grated as it turned, and she slithered feetfirst out the window. The sill dug into her stomach while her feet dangled two feet above Uncle Henry's prized rose garden. Not the best position, but not as bad as getting accosted by strange men in the middle of the night. She wriggled farther over the windowsill and let go.

Rose thorns sliced at her calves, her thighs. She bit her bottom lip. Shit! That hurt. Well, that would teach her to wear a skimpy nightgown rather than the flannelette pajamas her mother had packed. She extricated herself from the grip of Tom Thumb, Uncle Henry's favorite rosebush, and limped toward Nikolai's house. Pique made her grimace and think in curses. Just her luck. Her first night alone, and she needed help. A great start to her bid for independence.

"She's not here."

Summer glanced over her shoulder and once again cursed her nightgown. The pale material stuck out like a Jersey bull in her mother's vegetable garden.

"She must be here."

She changed direction, heading to the rear of Nikolai's house. She stepped onto the verandah and almost fell through a broken board. Damn and blast.

"The window's open. Check the garden." The intruders' voices carried on the night air.

An open window beckoned, the sheer net curtains fluttering in the soft breeze. The voices moved closer, and panicked, Summer dived through the opening.

Something tackled her, sending her flying. She landed on her back in the middle of a mattress. The air hissed from her lungs as someone pinned her in place.

"Don't move," a harsh voice gritted next to her ear. A hand moved down her arm and across her chest, freezing when it came into contact with her breast. This time, the succinct curse didn't raise so much as an eyebrow. The body pressing her into the bed moved, but not enough for her to draw a good lungful of air. A bedside lamp switched on, and she blinked at the bright light.

"You." Nikolai glared down at her. "What the devil are you doing in my bedroom?"

She swallowed. His hand was warm, and she felt her nipple hardening under his touch. Humiliation at her body's betrayal made her tense even as she savored the spike of sensation.

"Um...would you mind taking your hand off my breast?" The way her nipple was cozying into his palm—talk about a newsflash. Nikolai this close was unnerving, especially since he was the enemy. She refused to imagine how good it would feel if he rearranged their bodies a fraction. Nope, she wasn't going there.

The furrow between his brows

deepened. "Isn't that what you're here for?"

The innuendo made her stiffen even more. "Someone's broken into Uncle Henry's house."

"Why didn't you say so?" To Summer's intense relief, he released her. "Have you rung the police?"

"No. I..." Summer's voice trailed off as she took in the broad expanse of his naked chest. Oops, naked all over. Her gaze jumped northward, but the vision of masculinity remained seared to her retinas. He looked so much better without clothes.

Nikolai rolled his eyes with the same masculine impatience her brothers exhibited whenever they thought her behavior stupid. "Never mind. Get in bed and stay warm. I'll take care of things."

He yanked on a pair of jeans and

limped from the room before she could tell him what she thought of his verbal pat on the head. The rumble of his voice from the other room told her he was ringing the cops. No way was she staying in his bed and missing out on the excitement. She sprang off the mattress. This was more adventure than she'd ever imagined, and it was only her second day in Auckland.

Summer crept down the passage, feeling her way cautiously through the dark and unfamiliar house.

"I told you to stay in bed."

She jerked as his warm breath tickled her ear. Oh, boy. Who'd have thought an ear was an erogenous zone? She bit her bottom lip, frowned then grinned as a brainwave struck. "I heard a noise outside the window."

Luckily, it was dark since she couldn't

lie to save herself. And her body was broadcasting lustful messages a blind man could decipher. Full participation in this adventure would distract her, help her gain a semblance of control—she hoped.

"All right. Stay with me." He slid through the darkness with the ease of a soldier on night maneuvers.

She blundered after him and kicked a table leg. The clatter and her squeak of pain made him curse. Huh, another new one to save for later—wait until the next time her brothers tried to tell her how to live her life. Her brilliance would stun them into silence.

"Can't you be quiet?"

"I can't see."

Another muttered curse. "Here." He seized her hand. "Hold on to me and keep up."

Summer felt a royal salute coming on until he attached her hand to the waistband of his jeans. When she touched warm skin, every militant urge stalled. Her fingers curled over the body-warmed denim, her senses reeling, her body humming—from toe-tips to the top of her head. Bits in between tingled and plunged and swooped like a high-speed lift traveling to the ground floor. Oh, boy.

He opened the front door and slid outside. She stumbled after him, her mind engaged on sensation, the way her silk nightgown caressed her curves, rather than the need to reconnoiter.

He stopped without warning. Summer plowed into his back and her nose jabbed his shoulder blade. A whoosh of air escaped her parted lips.

His hands snaked out, steadying and

preventing her from falling. "Mind the step. I haven't got 'round to fixing it yet."

The step? Her next intake of breath was a mistake. It was full of him. Sandalwood soap and Nikolai. A very combustible combination. Who'd have thought?

In the distance, a siren sounded.

"Help is on the way." Satisfaction oozed from his voice. "They've managed to get here quicker than I thought they would. The siren is a nice touch."

Huh? She shook away her confusion to focus on the important things. "Are the intruders still in Uncle Henry's house?"

"Can't you hear them?"

Um, no. She couldn't register anything except the thud of her heart. It was a wonder he didn't pick up the rapid tattoo with him standing so close and all. Her breath stalled. Did he realize his hand had slid down to her butt? It wasn't her most attractive feature and frankly, she possessed better places if he wanted to explore.

"Damn, they've heard the siren."

Summer turned her head in the direction he was looking. Two shadowy figures sprinted across her uncle's lawn, past the fishpond out front and disappeared around the corner of the house. Seconds later, a car engine roared.

"Smart," Nikolai muttered. "Look, they're going to drive back down the road as if they have every right. If they sped off, that would appear suspicious."

A car pulled into Nikolai's driveway. The siren stopped.

"Stay there."

Another order. Summer considered then decided she refused to take orders. The police would want to interview her.

After avoiding the hole, she stepped off the wooden deck.

Two men leapt from the car, and the three of them indulged in a complicated handshake followed by a round of shoulder clapping that would've flattened a normal person.

Nikolai grinned. "That was quick."

"I was at Jake's place," one of the guys said.

Summer came to a screeching halt. Her eyes narrowed on the group, and she must've made a sound. The two strangers whirled and their faces, tight and ready for action, gave them away.

They were not policemen.

Both tall. Both muscular. Both with dark hair and military bearing, they screamed SAS mates.

"Who's the babe?" Although the voice was soft, the words carried.

Nikolai sighed heavily. "I thought I told you to stay put?" He limped up the path and tugged her by the arm until she stood in front of him. Summer felt his body heat sear the length of her back. His arm wrapped around her as if he thought she might attempt an escape. Pressed to his body and with his arm weighing down on her breasts, she could hardly breathe. "This is Henry's niece."

There was a moment's silence before one of the men whistled. "Not a babe then?"

Nikolai's limbs tensed, his grasp tightening.

Summer struggled for freedom, and he released her the instant she wriggled. Enough. They couldn't pretend she was invisible. She was right in front of their eyes. "Are the two mutually exclusive?" she demanded, clicking her fingers.

"Of course not, ma'am," one of the men said.

She glared and stuck out her hand. "Summer, not ma'am."

"Jake," the man replied.

Interesting. His hand was as warm as Nikolai's but didn't produce the same tingles. A soft growl came from behind her, and Jake grinned as he liberated her hand.

The other man beside Jake claimed it almost instantly. "Louie. Pleased to meet you, Summer." Louie's low drawl held flirtation, and she felt an answering grin gather momentum.

"Louie."

Startled, her gaze snapped to Nikolai. His face bore a feral warning while his tone promised reprisal. Against what she didn't know, but Louie did and he heeded the caution.

"Shirt," Nikolai snapped.

Jake and Louie grinned at each other. They did the silent communication thing then Jake shrugged, whipped off his cotton shirt and held it out to her. She stared in confusion. What did they want her to do with it? Wash it?

"Hell." Nikolai grabbed the garment and thrust it against her chest. "Put it on before we drown in the drool." A snicker drew his wrath. "What?"

"Nothing," Jake said.

Nikolai nailed her with a glare. "We'll go and check Henry's house. Make sure they've gone."

Summer nodded, and once they moved off, followed them.

"Stay," Nikolai ordered.

She halted and frowned at the departing men before glancing over her shoulder. Nope, Nikolai didn't own a dog.

And she didn't have fur.

She crept down the footpath after the three men, careful where she placed her bare feet. Her body ached in interesting places, but no way was she missing a single bit of this adventure.

Chapter 3

The woman would drive a sane man to drink if she didn't entice him into bed first. How the hell had he ever thought her unremarkable? Jake and Louie hadn't missed a trick. He was the one slow on the uptake, which made this babysitting assignment a trickier proposition than his original suppositions. Especially, when he had the urge to run his hands over her breasts and down her body in a one-on-one investigation.

His cock twitched in agreement. He cast a furtive glance over his shoulder and cursed. Jake and Louie stilled.

"Problem?" Louie demanded in an

undertone.

Nikolai sighed. "Nothing. You two go ahead. I'll handle it."

Jake glanced back, the ever-present humor turning up into a flagrant grin. "The babe?"

"Henry's niece," he gritted out. The plan was to look after the girl, not get down and dirty as his cock was so busily ordering. He was a babysitter.

Louie smirked. "Whatever."

They slid away, blending into the darkness without another word while he backtracked to deal with Summer Williams.

"I'm not in the SAS so I don't have to follow orders." She folded her arms across her chest, and Nikolai couldn't help but notice her spectacular curves. The girl obviously ate well—no lettuce leaves for her. She'd look great decked

out as a fifties movie star, but naked—
Whoa!

"Button up the shirt," he ordered, averting his gaze and mentally ordering his body to cool it. Henry's niece was way out of his league. Too young. Too naïve. And probably a virgin to boot. "You'll catch a cold."

"I'm not in the army. I'm not part of your unit." Her blue eyes shot heavy artillery fire.

"Who said I'm SAS?"

"Uncle Henry."

Nikolai glided closer, right into her personal space, intimidation on his mind. He sucked in a deep breath while striving for calm. Mistake. Her delicate feminine scent teased him, distracted him.

Flowers.

Woman.

Bad move.

The boys were right. He was thinking babe. He struggled with concentration, resisting the urge to shuffle in the manner of a raw recruit. Damn, his jeans were starting to feel like a suit of armor. Think cold showers.

"Henry wouldn't tell you that." Shit, if he carried on like this for much longer she'd notice his body's reaction. In a desperate act of self-preservation, Nikolai pictured the gruff, no-nonsense Henry. It didn't help. He took a hurried step away from temptation.

"My brothers are SAS. I can spot a military man from a hundred feet away."

She sounded so ferocious she piqued his curiosity. He might be SAS, but he wasn't contagious. "What's wrong with the army? Henry's military."

"Don't you mean what's right with

them? Military men are bossy, opinionated, macho, pigheaded, think their way is the sole way, shoot first and ask questions later, scare away boyfriends— Did I mention bossy? All for my own good, of course."

Nikolai watched her impassioned face and couldn't prevent a laugh. "Why don't you save the character assassination for your brothers and Henry? Remember me? The man you ran to for help." Since she'd made her opinion clear, he'd keep out of her way, apart from the promised weekly check for Henry.

Yeah, he could do that. Better for both of them that way. Besides, Henry wouldn't appreciate the thoughts running through his head. Hell, any guy who dared to think of his niece like this—if he had one. His jaw flexed. That included Jake and Louie.

Hell, especially Jake and Louie.

She planted her hands on her hips, dragging his reluctant gaze to her curvy body. "The two men are gone. I want to see the damage then go to bed. I have a busy day tomorrow."

Disappointment surged through him as quick as machine gun fire. He'd liked the look of her in his bed. The feel of her...hell! Preservation kicked in big time. The girl was young—too young. How many times did he have to tell himself before the facts sank into his thick head? Besides, he'd failed with Laura. He'd lost both her and their baby.

No point making the same mistake twice.

He was committed to his job, and that didn't leave room for anything else. Once this bum knee mended, he'd be back in the thick of the latest war brewing.

"All right. We'll check the house then leave you on your own." He took her arm and guided her down the footpath to Henry's house.

The front door stood wide open. Nikolai heard Jake and Louie murmuring in low voices near Henry's study, so he knew it was safe for her to enter.

Nikolai directed her to Henry's study, which had been ransacked. Books dotted the carpet, ripped from shelves and tossed haphazardly to the floor. Broken glass from picture frames crunched underfoot, and a coffee table and chairs lay at drunken angles, carelessly overturned.

He halted in the doorway. "Your feet are bare. Watch the glass. I need to know if anything is missing."

"How can I tell with this mess?"

"Thieves usually take portable valuables. Electrical goods. Jewelry. Money. Do the best you can. Take one room at a time."

She wandered off so he limped over to Jake and Louie, skirting glass and a broken chair. "Point of entry?"

Jake eyed the direction in which Summer had disappeared. "They forced the laundry window."

Nikolai's nod was curt. "I doubt Henry keeps anything of military value here, but we can't dismiss it totally."

"Nothing obvious missing." Louie shrugged. "They've tossed the study and the bedrooms. Kitchen and dining room are intact. You gonna contact Henry?"

"Nah." Ribald amusement surfaced at the idea. He could hear Henry's curses already, and none of the language sounded printable. "I know better than to interrupt a man on his honeymoon. Once he gets back is soon enough."

Jake righted a chair and straddled it. "You want us to stay?"

The glint in his friend's eyes made Nikolai sober and edginess seep into his muscles. He straightened to face off with his mate. The attempt at intimidation didn't shift Jake's smirk. Finally, he decided to pretend ignorance. "You might as well head off. I doubt they'll be back tonight."

Louie leapt in to pick up the gauntlet. "You and the babe be okay on your own? You don't need chaperones?"

Jake chortled.

Nikolai bared his teeth but there was no amusement involved. "Thanks for coming. Appreciate the help."

The three men walked to the door together, his two friends still chuckling loud enough to scrape him the wrong way. Never mind that he'd lead the joking if it were one of them in the same position.

"How's the knee?" Jake asked.

"Better. I start physio next week."

The phone rang, and all three men froze.

Louie scowled. "Damn funny time for the phone to ring."

Nikolai headed inside at a jog, ignoring the pain signals traveling from his knee. The ringing ceased.

Louie followed. "Too late. She's answered it."

"Summer!" Nikolai hollered.

She appeared at the end of the passage, and he saw her pallor even with the distance between them. When she saw him, she ran toward him. An instant later, he held her trembling body in his arms.

"Who was it?" he asked, already suspecting the answer.

She shivered. "I don't know. They told me they'd be back."

Nikolai tightened his hold as if he could stop the shaking by sheer willpower. "Anything else?"

"He told me I wouldn't have guard dogs all the time."

Nikolai waved off his hovering mates. "Catch ya tomorrow."

Louie nodded. "Ring if you need us."

"I think Nikolai has things under control," Jake said deadpan.

Stone-faced, Nikolai indicated the door with a jerk of his head. "Good night."

Summer pulled away from him. "Thanks for the help."

Jake winked, his pretty face wreathed in a babe-mag smile. "Anytime."

Nikolai growled, and Louie chuckled without restraint.

Summer glanced at him, her eyes wide and blue. They shimmered in the light, and seeing that, he braced for an emotional outpouring. Hell, he hated weeping females. Laura used to excel at tears on demand. It'd taken him a while to catch on, but experience still hadn't taught him how to cope with the feminine emotion.

"Where did they get in?" she demanded.

He did a double take. Not a tear in evidence. Instead, fury vibrated through her, rage making her glow with an inner fire. "Laundry window."

"Would you mind boarding it up while I finish checking the rooms for missing items?"

"No problem." Bemusement shaded

his tone.

Her head dipped in a no-nonsense nod as she headed for the lounge.

A flash of tanned limbs drew his gaze. "What happened to your legs?"

She slowed and glanced down with indifference. "I jumped out my bedroom window. Uncle Henry's rose garden is below."

Nikolai swallowed. He was trained to deal with medical emergencies in the field, but it was different, worse somehow, seeing her injured. Angry scratches marred the creamy perfection of her calves. The right leg appeared worse. The scratches went all the way up her thigh, disappearing beneath the flimsy hem of her nightgown. Closer scrutiny showed protruding thorns. "That must hurt. Why didn't you say something?"

She lifted one shoulder in a shrug. "I'll live."

"Where does Henry keep the first-aid kit?"

"You sound like my mother. Stop fussing. I'll grab the kit when I've finished checking the rooms."

He didn't know whether to laugh or groan. The lady had enough prickles to rival a rose bush without borrowing from nature. "How are you going to remove the thorns by yourself?"

"I'll look in the mirror."

"Wouldn't it be easier if I did it?"

She eyed him with clear mistrust. "I am not letting you look at my butt."

Her trepidation fed his determination to follow through. "Seen one butt, you've seen them all."

"This is a stupid discussion." She took three steps into the lounge. "Let yourself out when you've finished in the laundry."

He blinked at her retreating form. It had been a long time since anyone dismissed him that way. "How do you know I wasn't involved in the break-in?" he asked in a soft voice.

She whirled to glare at him. "That's not funny."

"You don't know me."

"Is this a lecture? A life lesson? I might come from the country, but I'm not stupid. Uncle Henry trusts you, and that's good enough for me." She stormed past the den.

Nikolai stalked her, admiring the feminine roll of hips as she stomped. His gaze drifted to her stiff shoulders and returned to her butt. Nope. Nothing wrong with her curvy figure.

She paused to right a stool, and as she reached for the chrome leg, Jake's shirt and the nightgown rode up. Nikolai's breath hissed through his teeth.

"Right, that does it." He tore his gaze away and fixed it on her indignant expression. "Where's the first-aid box? Those scratches go all the way up your leg. They'll get infected if they're not treated."

She huffed hard enough to blow a lock of hair from her eyes. "You're not going to leave without a fight, are you?"

"Nope."

Stubborn, stubborn man. "I heard Uncle Henry ask you to watch me. Are you going to boss me around the entire time he's away? Personally, I think this is an extreme plan to see my naked butt."

She caught his blink and watched his mouth curve in a sensual grin. Her heart sped up without warning, and her face heated. She wanted to fan her cheeks but kept her hands clenched at her sides. "How old are you?"

"Twenty-nine, almost thirty."

Good, another black mark to add to the dreaded bossy factor. He was way too old for her. The article in Miranda magazine suggested a five-year age gap was good, and she agreed. Besides, she didn't want to tie herself to one man, and the more her family interfered, the more determined she was to have fun and make up for lost time. Clear relief at his advanced age made her chirp, "I'm twenty-two."

"Is the first-aid stuff in the bathroom?"

Stuck record. Clearly, he wasn't going to back down. "Yeah, in the bathroom cabinet. I'll get it."

"You'll need to lie down. Your bedroom is the best place."

No. Definitely not, especially when she pictured her single bed and the lineup of stuffed bears. She imagined Nikolai touching her, gazing at her rear end. She shuddered. That was a big fat no. Dirty laundry covered the floor, still lying where she'd tossed it earlier. Underwear... She shook her head emphatically. "I don't think so."

"God, you're stubborn. Just like Henry. No more arguing or I'll paddle your butt."

Right, that did it—underhand tactics required. She spun around and fluttered her lashes. "Oh, kinky. Sounds like fun."

They stared at each other until he cleared his throat, breaking the silent challenge flaring between them. "I'd be gentle with you."

A shiver rippled through her, and it had absolutely nothing to do with the temperature in the dimly lit passage.

"Yeah, but would you respect me in the morning?"

A bark of laughter escaped him, changing the harsh angles of his face to handsome. "I thought we'd established I'm too old for you to hone your skills on."

She forced herself to move. What the heck was wrong with her? She wasn't usually susceptible to a military man. "We discussed it, but I wasn't aware we'd come to an agreement." Oops, what had happened to the naïve country girl from Eketahuna? And the decision that he was too old for her?

Nikolai brushed past her, heading for the bathroom. She heard the bang of a cupboard as it closed, the slide of the medicine cabinet and the hitch of careful footsteps as he limped back. Her insides clenched in anticipation.

"This your room?"

She nodded, eyeing him warily. She wasn't going to let him look at her butt, was she?

"On the bed."

An order. She remained in the bedroom doorway. The room seemed smaller than she remembered and a lot messier. Her gaze darted to the filmy underwear littering the floor. The piles of bright, in-your-face colors lying on the green carpet reminded her of wildflowers. Not one pair of plain white granny pants in sight. She tried to take comfort from that fact.

"I wonder what they were looking for," she mumbled. Conversation. That was what she required—something to distract both of them. "Do you think they were after goods to sell because I haven't found anything missing yet? And 'they'll be back' sounds like a line from a second-rate movie."

Nikolai stepped over a turquoise-colored bra with barely a pause. "Don't try to change the subject. On the bed."

The unyielding jaw suggested it was useless to argue, while her innate common sense suggested she close her eyes and think of...England.

While she hesitated, he straightened the covers and gestured impatiently. She hesitated until he quirked a challenging brow in her direction. Finally, she huffed out a put-upon sigh and stretched out, facedown on the bed, her pulse rate racing.

Silence fell, and her senses jump-started into hyperdrive. The groan of the first-aid box snapped like rifle fire when Nikolai opened it, the rustle of plasters and bandages, the return volley.

The mattress depressed on one side as he sat beside her. Heat gathered in her face.

He was staring at her butt.

She just knew it.

The silk of her nightgown rustled as he raised the hem. Cool air brushed across the tops of her thighs.

"Hell, why didn't you say something earlier? That must hurt."

He was looking at her legs. Fingers curled into the duvet cover while she bit back a moan. Beneath the silk fabric of the nightgown bodice, her nipples tightened while liquid warmth between her legs made her heart stutter in distinct alarm.

His fingers trailed over her left calf and up her thigh. The emotion in her face sprinted downward and spread until her body burned with unrelenting heat. She squirmed inwardly. Thank goodness, he couldn't see her expression or witness how turned-on she was, how much she wanted to explore his delectable body in return. Despite her virginal state, she lacked nothing in the imagination department.

"Can you hurry the process?" She wasn't proud of the begging tone, but desperation left no room for dignity.

She heard him rummaging through the first-aid kit. A metallic clink.

"This will hurt," he warned.

Not half as much as her pride. His fingers skimmed her thighs again. She trembled. Please let him hurry. She didn't think she could take much more of this torture. Actually, the pain wasn't too bad. At least it helped her concentrate on something other than his touch.

"All done." The tweezers clattered

against the kit as he put them down. "A little antiseptic and you'll live. I'll check the scratches for infection tomorrow."

"I don't think so. One free look at my butt is all you get." She turned over and sat up, tugging the silk nightgown down as far as it would go. He had the gall to laugh—a low, sexy chortle that sucked at her insides.

"Will you be okay here for the rest of the night, or do you want to sleep at my house in case they decide to return?"

Her gaze shot to him. Exactly what was he offering? Sudden pressure in her lungs reminded her to breathe. "I'll sleep here." The flexing of his jaw indicated he intended to argue. "You gave me an option and I've answered. I'll be fine. Despite the phone call, I doubt they'll return tonight."

His hesitation urged her to assert

herself before he started pushing her around. "I'll lock the windows and doors."

"I'll stay here tonight," he informed her as if she hadn't said a word.

"In my bed?" To her immense frustration, her sentence ended on a squeak.

Nikolai glanced at the bed and back at her. His lips kicked up in a faint smile. "Does it look as if we'd both fit in this sorry excuse for a bed?"

"There's no need for sarcasm."

"I'll sleep in Henry's room."

"Fine. You're going to do what you want no matter what I say." She stalked to her bedroom door and arched her brows in a silent order for him to leave. He made no effort to depart, and she spelled it out bluntly. "Good night."

The instant he cleared the doorway,

she slammed her door shut. She heard a chuckle before his slow, uneven retreat. Good. He's gone.

As she picked up a hairbrush and a tube of lipstick, she shoved Nikolai from her mind or tried to. Everywhere she looked, she was reminded of him. The first-aid kit still sat on her bed. Used pieces of cotton wool and a tube of antiseptic ointment were in plain sight, the impression his body had made on her duvet jolted her back in time. Lord, she could even smell the spicy scent of his soap.

Summer stomped around her bed and picked up a discarded drawer. She scooped up piles of silky lingerie and dumped them inside. She gathered a pile of books the intruders had tossed on the floor, along with the ring binder containing her study notes. Once the room looked more habitable, she decided to attempt sleep. She crawled under the covers and flicked off the bedside lamp.

Ten minutes later, she was still wide-awake. She reached over and turned on her lamp. She'd read. That was what she'd do. She checked the shelf where she'd left her parcel, frowned then fished inside the straw basket by her bed. Ah-ha! She extracted a package wrapped in brown paper from amongst two others and the rest of the junk in her basket. Ripping it open, she smiled and turned over the first book. Her satisfaction faded. She pulled the second book from the parcel and scanned the title, then the third.

This wasn't her package.

These weren't her books.

A frustrated scream lodged in her

throat, but she bit down on her tongue and glared at a book on fly-fishing. She would've released the screech if it wasn't for Nikolai's presence.

A card fluttered free from one of the books. It read, Special order for Alistair Martin.

So much for the reading idea.

She groaned and hoped Alistair Martin appreciated her hot romances.

Chapter 4

Nikolai haunted her thoughts all day just as he'd inhabited her Technicolor dreams throughout the night. The naked visual in her memory combined with all the sexual how-to articles she'd read to produce a truly stunning fantasy.

Two people slow dancing, their arms wrapped around each other. She and the big, bad SAS man. Slowly undressing. Letting clothing fall to the carpet while they continued to move to the music, rubbing against each other, pausing to slide lips across each newly bared body part. Her breasts tingling as Nikolai slid his mouth across the upper slopes and curves then tugged at a straining nipple through the silky fabric of her lemon-colored bra. He pulled away, leaving a circle of wet fabric.

"Do you like that?"

Summer considered. "I'm not sure. You'd better do it again."

Nikolai laughed, his dark eyes gleaming. "We can't have that. A woman should have an opinion about something this important." And he bent his dark head again, sucking the tip of her other fabric-covered nipple into his mouth.

A sensation of heat engulfed her entire body. She gripped his shoulder. "I need... It might be better if I took this off. I wouldn't want you to get fluff-balls."

Two dark brows shot toward his hairline as he released her nipple to stare at her. "Fluff-balls?"

"Like fur-balls in cats."

"You know, I think you're right." His hand slid behind her back, and with a casual flick, her bra fell open. "While we're at it, maybe we should get comfortable. How does the bed sound? We can try the kitchen table next time."

Was he teasing? She tipped her head back to study his face, her pulse kicking up at the sensual promise in his slumberous eyes, his smiling lips.

The rest of their clothes dissolved. Suddenly, cool cotton sheets were at her back, and Nikolai leaned over her, his tanned fingers exploring her breasts. She stirred restlessly, her breasts aching for his touch. When he finally touched her nipples, he pinched them hard. The corresponding jolt between her legs made her cry out.

"I'm going to make you so hot for me

you'll beg," he whispered against her belly. "I'm going to make you wet and hungry. Your pussy is going to weep for my possession." He kissed her quivering belly and used his tongue to trace her belly button. "I'm going to lap your juices and tease your clit like this." His tongue darted inside her navel then he licked around the rim.

His demonstration hiked her pulse rate. Excitement and anticipation warred as his hands alternatively soothed and plucked her breasts, and his mouth explored her belly button. The juncture of her thighs ached. She writhed and squirmed as her hips lifted. Liquid honey flowed from her cleft.

Her breath caught as Nikolai moved lower, his hot breath stirring the short hair on her mound. His tongue traced the heart-shaped thatch, leaving a gleaming wet path in his wake.

Summer's legs splayed, and she lifted her hips shamelessly, silently begging for his intimate touch. She felt so wet. So needy.

Nikolai parted her legs even farther, baring her to his sight.

"You're wet for me." His breath washed against her swollen clit. He blew against the tiny nub, and an intense shiver racked her body. "But you haven't begged yet. Ask, Summer. Ask me to give you pleasure. Tell me what you'd like. My mouth. My cock." He looked up at her then, their gazes colliding. His dark eyes compelling, dominant and so heavy with heat and promise that another shudder swept her body. "Tell me you want me."

"Please, Nikolai. I need you inside me. Please ease the sweet ache. Nikolai. Please."

She'd woken tingling, shuddering and so hot that a slow, cruising finger across her engorged clitoris had thrown her headlong into a toe-tingling orgasm. Now she craved the real thing, with the original Nikolai instead of a dream figure.

Oh, yeah.

Flapping a hand in front of her hot face, she shoved a returned library book from her trolley onto the shelf. But she refused to replace her well-meaning family with a bossy boyfriend. She sighed in resignation. Perhaps she'd buy a copy of the magazine with the article about sex toys. Then she could make an informed choice in the adult shop she'd seen in Papakura. Sex toys were the way to go until she met a worthy man, one that wouldn't boss her around and lay down the law.

"Wake up, Summer," the head librarian snapped, appearing from behind the animal husbandry section. "You've shelved that book in the wrong place."

The thin, dark-haired woman plucked the hardcover from the section on agriculture and thrust it at her. "Find its correct home then you may leave. I trust you'll pay more attention tomorrow."

"Sorry, Mrs. Ferguson." Something else to blame on him. She shoved the tome on the science shelf and stomped off to grab her orange straw basket and car keys.

She hoped this Alistair Martin was home because she wanted her books. Needed them. It was enough to drive a girl to write her own romances. In fact, she'd started composing chapter one in her head last night. The idea would've worked if the hero hadn't morphed into Nikolai. Her character had appeared with a distinctive bossy streak along with a hot body. Suffice to say, her sleep had become restless.

Summer fired up her rattle-trap car and backed from the parking space. She needed her hot and steamy romances. Fly-fishing just didn't do it for her. After driving down Queen Street, she indicated and transferred to the lane heading for Parnell.

"Number fifty-five, fifty-seven... A restaurant? That can't be right." She glanced at the card again. Definitely fifty-nine. A vacant car park decided the situation. She zipped into the space, scooped up the books and exited her vehicle.

The restaurant was beautiful. Classy. At least to the eyes of a woman from small-town Eketahuna. Her heels clicked over the mocha-colored tiles and intricate mosaic insets until she stood in a reception area. Over to her left, there was a bar area with plush chocolate carpets and built-in leather seating. Two couples sat in a booth, drinks before them, while four businessmen stood at the bar.

A stylish woman appeared in front of her. "Hello. Table for one?"

"Yes, please." A drink was a good idea.

She followed the woman to a table in an outside courtyard. Cacti and succulents in ceramic planters were arranged around the cobbled patio. Red and green umbrellas provided shade while music with a Spanish vibe gave an exotic ambiance. She half expected a man in a swirling black cape with a rose clamped between his teeth to appear from next door.

The woman seated her and produced a menu. "Your waitress will be with you shortly."

"Thanks. Actually, you might be able to help. I'm looking for a man—" She paused at the expression on the woman's face and laughed. "That didn't quite come out the way I meant. I mean I'm looking for a particular man. Alistair Martin. I don't suppose you know where I could find him? I wasn't expecting a restaurant at this number."

The frown on the woman's brow cleared. "You mean Dare. You're in luck. He's in the office at the moment. Can I tell him your name?"

"Summer Williams."

"I'll let him know you're here."

A waitress took her order and reappeared with a plate of bread and dips along with Summer's orange juice.

While she waited for Dare Martin to appear, she amused herself people watching. A group of university students over to her right were flirting with each other. A blonde girl flicked her hair over her shoulder and smoothed the nonexistent wrinkles in her tight-fitting red top.

Summer drew in a breath, enlightenment making her grin widen—lots of meaningful eye contact and mutual smiling happening there. So, that was what the article meant by body preening.

"Miss Williams?"

Summer started at the interruption. The man bore an amused yet quizzical expression on his handsome face. "Oops, caught me eavesdropping," she said in chagrin. "Call me Summer."

Of course, she'd appear a fool in front of an eligible man. At least she hoped he was single because he pushed her hot buttons—an excellent distraction from her neighbor. Her gaze darted down his suit-clad body to his left hand.

No ring.

Of course, the lack of ring didn't mean he was free of feminine entanglements, but it was a step in the correct direction.

His teeth flashed, dazzling white, as he grinned. "I'm Dare Martin. May I join you?" He indicated the empty chair at her table.

"Of course." Her fingers rose to press the embarrassment from her cheeks. "You weren't meant to catch me doing something so uncouth. It's put me at a distinct disadvantage."

Dare's gray eyes twinkled. "It's refreshingly honest. I believe you wanted to see me. I hope you're not after a job because I leave the hiring to my manager."

"Oh, no. Nothing like that. I think I have something that belongs to you." She bent to hunt through her basket, pulled out the brown paper bag containing Dare's books and passed it to him. "I hope you have my books. It was a huge disappointment last night when I discovered I had the wrong parcel. I don't know how it happened."

Dare glanced inside the bag, a pleased expression on his face. "I think I could kiss you."

Summer's gaze traveled to his lips. He didn't mean that, did he? Because she liked the idea.

"I rang the bookshop this morning, but they were adamant they gave me the right books." He signaled a passing waiter and ordered a drink. "Would you like another drink?"

Summer nodded. "Thanks. I suppose it was rather a shock to get a parcel of romances when you expected fishing books."

"You could say that. Look, I appreciate you taking the trouble to deliver my books in person. I'm afraid your books are at my home, and I'm busy tonight. Why don't I deliver them to you tomorrow?"

Another night without a decent book. She groaned in frustration. Maybe it was time to purchase an e-reader, and she'd have to think of another activity to put Nikolai from her mind, even if that meant cleaning the oven.

"I don't suppose you're free tomorrow afternoon?" he asked, breaking into her thoughts. "I'd like to buy you lunch to repay your kindness."

That should do the trick. A date to help push Nikolai out of her head. "You don't need to do that."

"Of course I don't." His gray eyes flittered across her lips and rose to meet her gaze. "But I'd like to. How does midday sound? Actually, you'd be doing me a favor. I want to scope out a competitor, and I won't stick out as much if I have a dining companion."

"You know how to turn a woman's head." Her stomach tingled pleasantly as his gaze drifted across her face again. It felt as if he were touching her, kissing her lips.

Dare burst into delighted laughter. "What I meant to say was that your beauty will dazzle the waiters, and they'll be too mesmerized to pay attention to me in spy mode."

"Smooth." She flicked her French braid over her shoulder and grinned. Oh, this flirting thing was fun. "Very smooth. I'd love to have lunch with you. Where are we going?" Under the table, she crossed the fingers on her left hand, hoping he'd name a smart restaurant, somewhere to show off the brand-new outfit she'd purchased during her lunch break.

"There's a new restaurant opening on the banks of the Waikato River, toward Hamilton. Where do you live?"

Yes! She just hoped there wasn't too much silverware to bamboozle her. She made a mental note to check the etiquette books and brush up. "Not the Liberty Jones restaurant?"

"The very same."

Perhaps she should see if she could book a hair appointment too. "I live in Bottle Top Bay, near Papakura, so it's on the way. Number twenty. It's a big white house."

His gaze did a final cruise of her face before he checked his watch. "I need to get a move on, but I'll be counting the minutes until tomorrow." Dare rose and moved around the table until he stood by her chair. He picked up her hand.

Summer met his gaze and felt trapped like a butterfly in a web. She couldn't have looked away if she tried. Her stomach churned in excited anticipation, much like the time she'd sat in the front car of the roller coaster waiting for the ride to start.

Dare sobered, a flash of something indefinable flickering across his face before he bent to press his lips against the back of her hand. A quiver shot down her arm, and she bit back a sigh. Talk about romantic.

"Until tomorrow," he murmured.

She nodded dumbly. "Tomorrow."

He released her hand with apparent unwillingness.

"You won't forget my books, will you?" Oh, boy. Part of her wished he'd leave before she made a fool of herself and he rescinded his invitation. The other part wanted him to stay right where he was so she could practice her flirting.

Dare released her hand. "I won't forget, but you won't have much time for reading. I intend to keep you very busy." With a quick smile, he strode off without looking back.

Once he'd left, she gave up trying to appear poised and energetically fanned her face with the menu pinched off the next table. "Fancy that. No time for reading." She flapped the menu with renewed vigor. "Be still my heart."

The last week had flown. Summer parked her car in Uncle Henry's driveway and leaned over to grab a pile of shopping bags. Today, during her lunch hour, she had made another serious dent in her savings account.

"Making up for lost time," she sang, doing a little shimmy as she exited the car. As she slammed the door shut, one of the bags slithered to the concrete footpath. "Bother."

"Let me," a husky voice said from behind her.

Nikolai.

She froze for an instant, knowing he'd come to check on her. Resentment flared, but she tamped it down. Nikolai had waved if he saw her but had kept his distance. Perhaps she shouldn't prejudge him today since he didn't appear to be taking the babysitting gig too seriously.

"Thanks." She indicated the bulging bags with a jerk of her head. "I've been shopping."

"What have you done to your hair?"

Summer juggled her shopping parcels so she could turn to look at him. Holy cow. One look at his face and her instincts screamed danger. She swallowed but refused to look away. "I had it cut."

"I can see that." He sauntered closer and picked up a lock of her hair between two fingers. He fingered the curl with care. "It's blue."

"I have blue highlights." Summer found she had to swallow again. "They go with my eyes."

Their gazes met and held. Summer felt

the leap of her pulse and knew she had to do something before she melted at his feet.

"You're the babysitter, not my father." Not that she ever in a million years imagined a parent who looked like Nikolai.

His mouth twisted. He released her hair and stepped back. "I feel old enough to be your parent."

Summer let that one go, while silently reminding herself she was interested in Dare. Nothing about Nikolai attracted her in the slightest. "Did you want something? I have a date, and I'm running late." She glanced at the oversized watch on her wrist. "Very late."

Nikolai retreated again, putting even more distance between them. His face had frozen, wiped of every emotion. She had no idea what he was thinking and suddenly she wanted to know.

"Just checking to see you haven't had any problems since the other night. Don't let me keep you."

"No problems. Not one." Summer crossed the fingers of one hand behind her back to negate the small fib. No problems that was, except the phone caller who specialized in heavy breathing. If she told Nikolai, he'd take over, and the little freedom she possessed would go poof. She heard the sound of a car approaching and wrinkled her nose. "Bother. That's Dare now."

"Go and do whatever you need to do. I'll tell the boyfriend you're running late."

"Thanks." She sprinted for the door, then came to a sudden halt and spun to glare at him. "Don't interrogate him."

"I don't have to stay. I have things to do."

Now she'd offended him. "Sorry. I—Never mind. Thank you. I'd appreciate you staying. Tell Dare I'll be ready in fifteen minutes."

Nikolai watched her race through the front door, not even stopping to unlock the door because she hadn't secured it when she left this morning. A snort escaped. Naïve. Innocent. He shook his head as he caught a flash of blue right before she disappeared, and this time a smile tugged at his lips.

Blue hair.

She was right about one thing—it did match her eyes.

Behind him, the car pulled up. He leaned against the fender of Summer's battered Mazda and watched the driver climb from the late-model BMW.

He hated him on sight.

Dare was a city man, slick and

well-groomed in his fancy duds—a suit no less, even in the humid summer weather. Nikolai scanned his worn jeans and paint-splattered T-shirt and shrugged. Why the hell was he comparing himself with the bantam rooster? His job was to keep an eye on Summer.

That was all.

He pushed away from the car, stood to his full height and held out his hand. "You Summer's date?"

The guy nodded but didn't accept the welcome.

"Nikolai Tarei," Nikolai said. "Summer's running late. She'll be out soon." His brows rose since the man continued to stare at his outstretched hand. Yeah, it was covered with paint, but that was because he'd been painting.

Finally, when he was ready to give up,

the suit flashed an insincere smile and accepted the greeting. "Thanks. I'm a bit early. I'm Dare Martin."

The suit's hand was soft and pampered. What the hell did Summer see in him? He was pretty enough. Had a few bucks in his back pocket, if the car was any indication. But Henry wouldn't approve, and from Summer's mentions of her two brothers, he guessed they'd have problems with her date too.

"You related to Summer?"

Nikolai retreated to lean against the car. He folded his arms across his chest and looked him in the eye. "No."

"Hi, Dare! Sorry I'm so late. The meeting went late after work and the traffic at Spaghetti Junction crawled." The nasty glare she sent him told him she'd overheard. She sauntered up to Dare and stretched up to plant a kiss on the man's lips. Oh, yeah. Her disapproval beamed loud and clear.

Martin's hands curled around her waist with a possessiveness that Nikolai would need to be blind to miss. A roaring protest filled his mind, screeching for release. His hands dropped to his side and fisted.

Son of a bitch.

What the hell was the girl wearing? He scrutinized the long expanse of tanned leg beneath the hem of the tight black skirt, the strappy heels on her feet. Then his gaze lifted and paused to savor the two inches of creamy skin at her waist before he hit cloth again. What had happened to the baggy sack thing?

When she turned to face him, his mouth emptied of every trace of spit. Her black top was sheer and lacy. And low. His gaze fastened on the swell of luscious curves before he had time to veto the action. She might be years younger than him, but she was fully grown. Not a shred of doubt there. He forced his gaze northward to meet the challenge in her blue eyes.

"Ready to go, sweetheart?" Martin asked.

Summer nodded. She allowed the clotheshorse to place his arm around her waist, his fingers to skim over her bare flesh. The hair at the back of Nikolai's neck prickled until he felt like a Doberman guarding its territory. He wanted to rip her from Martin's arms and attack. Summer was his and he—

Whoa!

His thoughts screeched to an appalled halt. Where the hell had that come from? He was useless at male-female interaction. Laura had told him often enough. Every time Laura had needed him, he'd let her down, usually because of his job, which was why he was keeping away from relationship stuff. He shook his head to clear a sluggish brain, pounding with regrets at past mistakes. Dammit, Henry shouldn't have given him this assignment.

Martin escorted Summer to the passenger side of his black BMW and helped her inside before closing the door. From where he stood, Nikolai got a free showing of smooth thighs and fire-engine-red panties. He'd be willing to bet Martin received the same view.

Martin offered a curt nod in his direction before rounding the BMW and climbing into the driver's seat.

Nikolai scanned the registration plate and committed the number to memory. He wanted to tell Summer not to be late home, but dumped the thought before he uttered the damning words. That might be taking his duties a little too seriously. The blue sedan he'd seen driving up and down the road might belong to one of the neighbors or a visitor. Probably nothing worthy of worry.

Summer grinned at the clotheshorse, and Nikolai felt the instantaneous tightening of his gut. The man returned her friendliness, but his eyes didn't smile with genuine emotion, and his expression didn't quite match his curving mouth.

Instinct kicked in, making Nikolai tense. Something wasn't right. He wrenched his gaze from the man's hand pawing Summer and concentrated on Martin. A growl built in his throat.

Hell, who was he trying to fool?

It was good, old-fashioned jealousy at its most simplistic. Ever since he'd seen her in that silky nightgown, his thoughts had veered into dangerous territory. No matter how many cold showers he took, the memory stubbornly remained. Perhaps he needed a night on the town with Jake and Louie—along with some feminine company.

He needed to get laid.

The low rumble of the motor jerked him from his reverie. Forcing a grin, he lifted his right hand in farewell. The clotheshorse reversed his car and took off in a spray of gravel. Summer never looked back.

Nikolai's smile faded the second the BMW disappeared. He shoved away from the Mazda and limped up the path to his house. Time for a few phone calls—a little private investigation. He didn't have to take action, but at least the edgy sensation that kept the hairs on the back of his neck rising to attention would subside.

He'd promised to look after Summer, and he'd be failing if he did anything less.

Nikolai paced the length of his moonlit kitchen and peered out the window for what seemed like the hundredth time. He checked his watch. The hands glowed in the dark and told him the bloody thing was still working as five minutes had elapsed since the last time he'd checked.

Summer wasn't home.

It was after midnight, closer to one. What the hell kind of time was this for a date to go to? Surely, she'd arrive home soon?

He hobbled another circuit of his

kitchen before freezing like a leopard scenting prey. What if she wasn't coming home? What if she intended to spend the night with the clotheshorse?

He cursed low with feeling. He'd told Henry this babysitting lark was a mistake. Maybe he'd have to start searching for her. As he grabbed his keys, a car pulled up outside.

About bloody time.

He strode to the window to peer between the slats of the blinds. The BMW idled in Henry's driveway. From his vantage point, he watched two silhouettes merge into one. Instant fury had his fists balling, and he took two steps toward his front door before he realized confrontation was a mistake.

Look at her earlier reaction when the clotheshorse had come to pick her up. She'd kissed Martin because of his behavior.

Nope, he needed to approach this situation with stealth. He glared at the single silhouette. God, how long could one kiss take? His hands gripped the windowsill. They'd need to come up for air soon.

He snapped his eyes shut, blocking the sight. If he played the voyeur much longer, he might rush out there and drag her from the car. He counted to ten, dredging for control and deeper again for patience.

Catch-22. Damned if he did and damned if he didn't.

His eyes opened again. Ah, that was better. He loosened his grip on the windowsill and flexed his fingers.

The passenger door opened, and she slipped from the car. Nikolai's heart thudded anxiously. Was Martin going to stay at Henry's tonight?

The car started, and Nikolai released the breath. Every instinct screamed at him to go to her, but he didn't.

She was safe.

Best he keep his distance, or else they'd really be in trouble.

Chapter 5

Summer hummed softly as she padded around the kitchen. She plugged in the coffeemaker and poured a spoon of batter into a hot frying pan. The melted butter sizzled as the pancake mix hit the pan, and the scent of freshly ground beans filled the air along with the audible drip, drip, drip of the coffee into the carafe.

A thump on the front door brought a frown.

"Come in," she called.

Once the small air bubbles in the batter started to pop, she deftly flipped the pancake to cook the other side.

"The front door wasn't locked."

She grimaced. Nikolai, of course. "And a good morning to you too."

"The front door wasn't locked." His voice rose to a dull roar.

She sighed, removed the pan from the heat and turned to face his wrath. "I heard you the first time."

"This isn't Eketahuna."

Summer glanced out the kitchen window at the gulls flying lazily over the estuary. "It's not crime central either."

"You had a break-in the other night. God." He dragged a hand through his hair, negating his prior use of a comb.

He looked...sexy and very jumpable with that just-out-of-bed look and the dark stubble shading his jaw.

"Are you listening to me?"

Oops. He was starting to sound like her brothers. Best she pay attention. "Sure, I'm listening. The door wasn't unlocked all night. I've been out for a walk this morning." She picked up a plate and slid the pancake from the pan. "It's a lovely day. Want breakfast?"

"Stop changing the subject."

Okay, so he was a bit smarter than her brothers, but that didn't mean he could boss her around. "I realize you're watching out for me, but you don't have to guard me 24/7. I'm not stupid. The door was locked while I was out last night. The door was locked overnight. Subject closed. Would you like some breakfast?"

He scowled. "Is that coffee I smell?"

"Sure is. Help yourself while I finish cooking the pancakes. Do you know where the cups are?"

"Yeah."

She turned back to the stove. Funny, since his arrival, edgy awareness replaced her prior cheery satisfaction. Her heart raced, her mouth felt as dry as unconditioned hair and her nerves twitched. The sensation was quite different to what she experienced when she was with Dare. Interesting. She peeked over her shoulder, took a second to admire his jean-encased butt then flipped her pancake. What was it about this man that made her thoughts turn to sex?

She knew without even thinking that becoming more involved with Nikolai was a mistake. He was bossy, and she'd trade one prison for another.

"Do you want coffee too?"

He spoke from right behind her and she started. The man prowled, creeping up on a woman without warning. She sucked in a deep breath to resettle. "Please. White, no sugar."

Summer turned her attention back to cooking. Pour, cook, flip. Simple, except if your hands shook. The bubbles popped, and she flipped too vigorously. The pancake landed half in the pan and half on the element.

"Damn." She tried to retrieve the pancake without mangling it too much.

"Can I help?"

Summer whirled to nail him with a glare. "Quit sneaking up on me. You're not on maneuvers now." She used her spatula to point at a wooden chair. "Sit."

"Yes, ma'am."

Her eyes narrowed. "Stop that. What are you doing here anyway? I thought all you needed was a visual."

The man squirmed—he actually stirred uneasily and refused to meet her gaze. Her antenna shot to high alert.

"What?" Summer tapped her right foot

on the lino floor. Slap, slap, slap.

A trace of red appeared high on his cheekbones. She would've bet his ears turned red as well, but since his hair covered them, she couldn't confirm. He rolled his shoulders in a nonchalant shrug. His attempt at casual didn't fool her.

She advanced on him, waving her spatula like a weapon. "What have you done?"

His broad chest lifted as he dragged in air and momentarily distracted her. She mined her imagination for ideas on what he'd look like without the body-fitting T-shirt, but when she felt the lick of heat through her body, she called up something cold. Icy cold to cool the latent heat that shot to her pussy.

She needed to check out some toys since she refused to jump into bed with just anyone to soothe a healthy sex drive. Well, at least, she thought she was normal. With two guard-dog brothers, a sex life was downright difficult.

"I called in a few favors to get the clothes—ah, Martin investigated."

"You did what?" The end of her sentence came out as a shriek, but she was too incensed to care. "Why?" She waved the spatula in front of his nose and missed by a whisker.

He erupted from his chair, grabbed her upper arms and wrestled the implement from her grip. Incensed, she kicked him in the shin. Hard.

The next minute, she was plastered against his chest with both of them breathing harshly. Her breasts squashed against the planes of his chest, and the slumbering inferno inside her roared to life again. Her nipples peaked against her silky shirt. The physical reaction brought irritation at herself. She fought to escape, squirming and wriggling.

"Let go." The brute. How dare he manhandle her? How dare he interfere in her private life? Her love life was none of his business.

He settled the dispute by yanking her even closer so she felt every muscle in his body, all the way down. She froze and mortified color heated her cheeks. She would not look down. She would not look down.

Summer looked down.

His cock bulged in his jeans, showing she wasn't the only one with a sexual appetite. A gasp escaped, and the fiery heat in her face escalated.

He chuckled—a smug masculine sound. "Yeah. Now, if I let you go, are you going to behave yourself?"

She gave a clipped nod, and he loosened his hold. She promptly balled her hand into a fist and plowed it into his stomach. The air exploded from his lungs with a satisfying hiss.

"That's for being nosy," she snapped.

An instant later, she was plastered against his muscular frame. His lips moved and she realized he was speaking. She tried to hold on to her righteous anger, tried to concentrate, but she had trouble ripping her gaze from his beautiful lips. Heck, who'd have thought she'd find his mouth so interesting, since it mostly growled at her.

"Are you listening?"

Her head wobbled with the force of his shake. "It's a little difficult if I can't breathe. I'm starting to feel light-headed." It was his proximity. His cock dug into her belly. Gave a woman all sorts of interesting ideas. She traced his lips with her gaze. Would they feel soft? Hard? Or somewhere in between? Did she dare kiss him? All in the name of research, of course.

Summer stretched up on tiptoe even as she formulated the thought and pressed her lips to his. He froze, and she laughed inside, delighting in his reaction.

Flummoxed.

A surprised soldier.

Her arms crept behind his head, her fingers running through the silky strands of his hair. He groaned and took over the kiss. Which was a good thing since she'd reached the upper limits of her experience.

She felt the steady thud-thud-thud of his heart. His hands smoothed their way from her upper arms to cup her face, and she realized she was no longer held captive, that she remained plastered against him of her own volition.

His tongue flicked across the seam of her lips, traced her bottom lip, her top. Corny though it was, fireworks exploded behind her closed eyes. Bright flashes of orange and blue, electric yellow and fiery red burst inside her mind.

"Open your mouth," he murmured, low and husky.

Oh, yeah. That's what Miranda magazine had recommended. She surrendered to the suggestion and tasted the vanilla spice of her favorite coffee along with the heady taste of him. His tongue delved into her mouth, thrusting and parrying then retreating.

Summer trembled. Lordy. Miranda knew their stuff. This was absolutely the best part…so far. She tried to recall the next step, but it was too difficult to concentrate. Going with the flow seemed easier.

Nikolai froze when she moaned. Hell, he had his tongue down her throat. How the hell had that happened? He eased back but wasn't able to stop himself having another quick sample of her top lip. Hell, she tasted good. She felt good too—soft in all the right places. No bony hips on this woman. Just lots of luscious curves…

He dived in for one last kiss before he eased away with regret. His gaze lingered on her lips. They were red and glistened from his kisses. For a moment, he was tempted to shove away good sense and kiss her again, then guilt let rip with a swift kick to his conscience.

Get a visual, Henry had said. So what did he do? He went one better and copped a feel.

Fuck.

Age wasn't just slowing down his body. It was affecting his brain.

He plastered his hands firmly to his sides. "I...ah..."

Summer sauntered over to the stove. As he studied the sway of her hips, he tried to untangle the knots in his tongue.

Apologize.

Promise her it wouldn't happen again.

She turned to beam at him. The knots in his tongue turned on themselves, creating double knots. In the end, he gave up, and watched her instead. He'd never been one for talking anyhow. He was the action type.

"You ready for the pancakes?"

"Yeah. Thanks." Had she forgiven his

nosing around in the clotheshorse's background? He studied her carefully. Her mouth wore a soft, sexy smile but when their gazes collided, he noted a steely hardness in her blue eyes.

The same expression he witnessed in his own mirror when about to embark on a mission—determination and the grit necessary to get the job done. Nikolai broke the connection. He wasn't going to bring up Martin first. He'd wait for her to raise the subject.

He hobbled to the sturdy wooden table at the far end of the kitchen and sat on the closest chair, glad to take the weight off his knee. He picked up his coffee mug. The table bore a cloth these days. One of Veronica's little touches, along with pots of herbs on the windowsills. Henry's life was in for more changes, but somehow Nikolai didn't think he'd worry.

He'd never seen a man so smitten.

Summer pulled a heaped plate of pancakes from the oven.

"Do you want me to set the table?"

"No, stay there."

She was pure feline grace as she strolled toward him. A groan built in his throat. Fuck, he was toast if Henry discovered he'd stuck his tongue down her throat. And perish the thought if he ever learned of his latest fantasies.

The plate of pancakes dropped lightly to the table, then another platter of crispy bacon. She turned away and headed for the pantry. Her hips swayed in a pert wiggle that made him desperate to explore those curves in greater detail. She returned with a jar of maple syrup and caught him in the act. Instead of acting flustered, or shy or embarrassed, she winked.

Winked, by God.

His brain changed from park to drive in two seconds flat, and he half rose from his chair. A second later, he hit reverse with a loud shriek of brakes. He dropped back to the padded cushion with a soft thud. Something akin to shock ricocheted through the rational part of his mind.

Summer was years younger than him—still a babe in terms of experience. He had no business kissing her, no business lusting after her. Every relationship in his life so far, from the parental one to Laura had failed. Hell, even his latest mission. It was best if he didn't leave the starting gates this time. In the future, the visuals he'd promised Henry would suffice. He'd treat Summer Williams like a no-fire zone and keep his hands off.

But even as he made the decision, he couldn't tear his gaze from the sway of her hips under the black denim skirt, and before he even gave it a second thought, his gaze moved on to her rounded breasts. Whoa—no bra.

Someone ought to give that girl a good talking to. He swallowed, opened his mouth and shut it again so quickly his teeth clunked. He averted his gaze. He was not going there. He'd eat breakfast, say his piece about Martin and leave her to do what she would with the intel.

After Summer brought up the subject.

She slid an empty white plate in front of him and handed over a knife and fork. She dropped into the chair opposite and stretched out her legs under the table.

Nikolai jolted at the brush of her limbs and thanked God he hadn't gone with a pair of shorts. He resettled his legs and exhaled.

"Bacon?"

He nodded. Instead of handing him the plate, she speared a piece of bacon with a fork and leaned toward him to place it on his plate. Her flimsy blouse gaped at the neck, exposing creamy curves. Spectacular, mature curves with dusky nipples. His gaze fixed with superglue intensity. A whoosh of heat suffused his body, muscles tightened all over, in places that had no business reacting. His cock ached as blood pooled low, priming him for action.

"Ah, that...that's enough bacon."

She beamed, an innocent siren's smile that wound his insides so tight he thought he might shatter.

"How many pancakes?"

Nikolai nodded.

The siren's smile brightened,

beckoning him closer, luring him and creating havoc of his earlier resolutions. Damn, he wanted to play so much his hands shook.

She laughed softly. "I'll give you two to start with."

This time she picked up a pair of tongs and deftly transferred the pancakes to his plate. He caught another glimpse of her breasts, and his dick tightened with painful intensity.

He grasped the wrist holding the tongs. "Stop it."

"What?" The smile that bloomed was innocent, but the glint in her blue eyes didn't come close.

Nikolai's gaze was snared again by the rise and fall of her breasts. "You know what I mean," he snapped. "Don't do it."

Ohhh! This was fun. Summer fought

the blooming grin with all she had. His hand shackled her wrist, holding her firm, yet he tempered his strength, not inflicting pain. She stared into the swirling depths of his dark eyes. Her breasts tingled when she faced the stormy heat burning in his gaze. She moistened her bottom lip, reliving the taste of him, the sensation of his mouth against hers.

Then she closed one eye in another wink. "Would you like syrup with that?"

Nikolai swore, his curse another original. She took a mental note to keep it for the next time her brothers tried to interfere in her life.

"Martin's family is involved in crime." The statement was delivered in a flat tone as he released her wrist. He leaned back in his chair and waited.

"A crime family? What do you mean?"

"His family fronts an organized crime ring. Stay away from Martin. He's bad news." He picked up the bottle of maple syrup, drizzled it over his pancakes and calmly began to eat.

Summer blinked. She should be angry, but he wouldn't make up this stuff. Truth and honor radiated from him. She glanced at his bent head and frowned as he crunched on crispy bacon. "Nikolai, I'm not stupid. If I had the slightest clue Dare was involved in something illegal, I'd run a mile. You can't tell me he's part of a crime family and not give me details. Spill."

"You told me not to interfere." He cut into his pancakes with a precise incision that would have done a surgeon proud. His jaw moved as he chewed stoically, ignoring her questions.

Her hands tingled with a mighty urge

to hit him or at least seize him by the shirt and give him a good shake until answers spilled forth. Cripes, and men thought women were unpredictable. She reached over and made a grab for his hands. "Stop."

Dark brows rose, but he didn't pretend innocence. "I can't tell you where I got the intel, but the source is good."

She gritted her teeth. Shaking was looking good. "What else did they say?"

"Rumor is that Martin has taken over from his father and is intent on putting his stamp on the business."

"He's a restaurateur. The family owns several restaurants in the Auckland region."

Nikolai picked up his knife and fork. "Good places to launder money."

"All right. Say the rumors are true. Why haven't the police done anything?"

"Because they're too clever to get caught."

An idea sprouted. She tossed it around, considered it from several angles and decided it was a keeper. "I wonder if the police have anyone undercover."

His eating utensils clunked onto his plate. His hand whipped out to snare her right wrist and her attention. "Don't even think it. It's a damn-fool idea."

"But if the man's a criminal—"

"No." His eyes were hard, his expression flat.

Big, bad SAS man mode. She glanced pointedly at her shackled wrist. "Are you going to let me go any time soon?"

Nikolai dropped her wrist as if he'd been scorched by fire. "Henry should have locked you up. Throwing away the key would've worked too."

Summer glared back. "He did the next

best thing—he gave me you." And thank the Lord he did. Teasing Nikolai got the adrenaline going, her own personal energy drink.

Nikolai scowled. "So we agreed. You're not going to see Martin again."

Okay, enough was enough. "I enjoy Dare's company. He's a gentleman."

"Maybe my manners and clothes could use a bit of work, but at least with me, what you see is what you get."

Summer gave up trying to eat. "I can't ditch Dare without a good reason."

"Women do it all the time."

"I'm not most women."

Nikolai rolled his eyes. "Hell, you're not wrong there. No wonder Henry wanted a babysitter."

"Look, Dare and I have gone out a couple of times. So what? We're just friends. Unless I see proof with my own eyes, I'm going to keep seeing him."

"From what I saw, you're more than friends."

Summer stilled. "What are you talking about?"

"The lip-lock last night."

"Were you spying on me?"

Nikolai avoided her glare. "I was worried."

"I should point out we were lip-locked not long ago."

The instant the words left her mouth, the air in the kitchen thickened. Awareness pulsed between them, and Summer couldn't have looked away from him under threat of gunfire. Every part of her body ached for his touch.

"That was a mistake."

She shrugged. "Didn't feel like one to me."

After two beats of pregnant silence,

Nikolai shot to his feet. "I've got to go."

"Running away?" Summer asked in her sweetest voice.

"It's the right thing to do."

She didn't agree but didn't argue the point. "Whatever." She watched him hobble from the kitchen, and once he reached the door, she said, "I'll let you know if I need help with my investigation."

He whirled so quickly, he almost caught her grin before she wiped her expression clean. His glare was dark, his eyes stormy as he snarled, "Over my dead body."

Chapter 6

"I think that went well," Summer remarked to Joe, Veronica's pudgy, black cat.

The slam of the door made them both stare in that direction, then Joe returned to his grooming schedule. She pulled a face and stood to clear the half-eaten remains of their breakfast.

The phone rang just as she was drying her hands.

Her insides did a shimmy at the familiar voice. "Hi, Dare. I enjoyed last night."

"I did too." His smoky voice slid down the line, smooth as expensive brandy. "What are you doing today? I forgot to ask last night."

Good timing. She wanted to start her investigation straightaway. She checked her watch. "I've got a Tae Kwon Do lesson this morning, but apart from that I don't have anything planned."

"How does an afternoon at the beach sound and a barbecue afterward?"

"Sounds great."

"Good. My family has a bach at Maraetai Beach. You'll meet my two brothers and three sisters."

Summer did a silent high-five on hearing the invitation to visit their holiday home. She couldn't have planned things better. Once she met Dare's family, she'd have an idea of what to do next. "What time?"

"How does two sound?" He paused. "Why don't you bring an overnight bag in case the barbecue runs late, hmm?"

"But—" The phone went dead before

she finished. If Nikolai was right, she wouldn't get involved any further with Dare. And she certainly wasn't going to sleep with the man. "Well, doggone it. What am I going to do now? And how am I going to get past my guard dog?"

Sashay, with her nose in the air.

That was how she managed the task. Nervous tension bubbled in her tummy and choked her throat, pushing for freedom in the form of a hysterical giggle. But she made it to the car in one piece despite his black glower.

"Does that man always glare?" Dare asked as he seated her in the passenger seat of a black sports car.

"Afraid so," she said cheerfully. Now that she was inside the car, she felt marginally safer. "Just ignore him. I do."

The car started with a throaty purr.

Summer turned her attention to the soft, butter-colored upholstery. "I've never driven in a convertible before. Does this car belong to you too?"

"What do you think? It's new. I picked it up this morning. You're my very first passenger."

"I love it." She gestured at her old, dented car. "I'm obviously in the wrong business."

"Stick with me, sweetheart, and we'll go places." As he spoke, he reached out and squeezed her bare knee. "My family is looking forward to meeting you."

"I'm looking forward to meeting them too." And asking all sorts of questions. Her family might be overprotective, but they'd taught her a thing or two about interrogation.

"So, have I kept you too busy to read

your romances?"

Summer tucked a strand of blue hair behind one ear. "I've read one." In the middle of the night, to take her mind off Nikolai.

"How often do you get to the bookshop on High Street?"

She saluted at Nikolai as they sped off. She imagined his expression but refrained from glancing back to check the depth of his disapproval. "Once or twice a week. It's not far from the library. They stock a lot of my favorite authors."

"Romance," he teased with a sideward glance, as he paused at a give way sign.

"You're as bad as my brothers. I like reading romance, and I refuse to apologize for my habit."

"I don't get to the shop often. I usually ring my orders through and get someone to pick them up for me."

"If you need anything collected let me know. At least if I do it, you won't end up with the wrong package." She tossed him a smile while her mind worked at hyper-speed. So far, so good. Tomorrow, after her Tae Kwon Do class, she'd mine books from the library for help. She was bound to pick up a few investigation hints from Stephanie Plum.

Nikolai couldn't believe the woman. Given his threats, he'd thought the clotheshorse would be history. Obviously, he was losing his touch.

He was definitely losing his mind.

He headed for his kitchen at a lope and mentally thanked his Hitler-wannabe physiotherapist for pushing him. The knee was starting to feel as though it belonged to him again. He grabbed his phone and keys then raced for his car. Two seconds later, he returned to snatch a cap. He jammed it on his head and hustled back outside.

Gravel spat as he reversed from his garage and shot down the road on the heels of Martin and Summer. The speedometer edged upward. He jabbed a button on his phone and held it to his ear while he negotiated a corner.

"Yo."

"Louie, it's Nik. Remember that guy I had you run a check on?"

"Yeah."

"Do you remember if he has a beach house?" The beach was a safe bet. Summer had carried a bright-colored towel in the top of that orange basket of hers, and she'd been wearing shorts. Nikolai swallowed at the memory. Brief shorts that had highlighted her long legs.

He imagined them entwined around him—

"No beach house."

Damn. "What about his family?"

The clear tap of fingers on a keyboard filtered down the phone line. Nikolai was coming up to the motorway turnoff. He'd have to decide which way to go. "Hurry up," he muttered.

"Jeez, man, I heard that. I'm the one doing you a favor."

Chastened, he apologized. "Sorry." He slowed the car as he approached the turnoff. Still no sign of the black car. Which way should he go? They could have gone to any number of beaches around Auckland.

"The parents own a waterfront house at Maraetai."

"Yes!" Nikolai zipped past the motorway turnoff toward Papakura.

"Where? What's the street number?"

Louie rattled off the details.

"Thanks, Lou. I owe you."

"I wouldn't mind a day at the beach. Jake and I will meet you there."

Nikolai grinned as the phone clicked in his ear, and he turned the car toward Clevedon and Maraetai beach.

Summer burrowed her bare feet into the sand and small, pulverized shells. She leaned back on her elbows, lazily grinning while the sun beat down from overhead. The sharp tang of coconut filled the air as Natasha, one of Dare's sisters, applied suntan lotion to her legs and arms.

"It's too bad Dare was called into work," Natasha complained.

"It doesn't matter. The problems

were unexpected. You saw his disappointment."

"But he's your boyfriend. Aren't you angry? I bet he didn't need to take my brothers and father with him too."

Summer idly surveyed the stream of people sauntering past their spot. "Dare and I are friends. We're not serious." Part of her was sorry she was alone and stuck with Dare's sister. There were some seriously good-looking bodies parading on this beach. Her gaze swept from the high-tide mark and back to the gently swishing waves surging and retreating. She adjusted her bikini top as her eyes came to a halt on the group of three men not far down the beach. Now that was some serious eye candy. Three bronzed bodies that came complete with the requisite muscles.

"You can't be just friends," Natasha

said. "Dare's never brought a girl here before. Have you slept together?"

Summer's head jerked in shock. "Natasha."

"Sorry. I guess that was a bit personal."

Summer hid her amusement. Natasha didn't sound the slightest bit sorry. "Yes, it was. But here's your answer. We've known each other for two weeks, and at twenty-two, I'm way too young to get serious about a man." Her gaze swung back to the group of three men. They'd stood and were wandering toward the water.

One wore a knee brace.

Summer bolted upright and grabbed for her flapping bikini top.

"What's wrong?"

"Nothing." That had better not be Nikolai. She tied the strings of her bikini in place and stood. After wrapping her sarong about her body like a suit of protective armor, she brushed the sand and shell fragments off her feet and thrust them into sandals. "I think that's someone from work. I'll just go and say hello."

"Where?" Natasha fastened her bikini top.

Summer pointed at the three men. "Down there at the waterline."

"They're going swimming. There's no point wearing your sarong and sandals."

Summer grimaced and stooped to remove her sandals. So, they'd all get an eyeful of her oversized curves. "Thanks."

As she strode off, the man in the knee brace dived into the water. It was Nikolai. She'd recognize that butt anywhere.

"I'm coming too," Natasha declared from behind her.

Summer stiffened at the predatory

interest in Natasha's voice. She didn't want anyone ogling Nikolai up close. "What will your brother say if he hears I've been introducing you to older men?"

Natasha fell into step. "If Dare had his way, I'd leave the house wearing a yashmak."

The sheer feeling in Natasha's words ruffled Summer's conscience. Her brothers were the same—heavy-handed with intimidation when it came to boyfriends. Sympathy rose in her. "Dare's an overprotective brother?"

"Oh, yes. Let me live a little, even if it's through you. And besides, you're what—two years older than me."

"Come on then. I'll introduce you, but don't tell Dare. If you do, I'll deny everything."

"Let's go in case Dare arrives back unexpectedly."

By the time they reached the water's edge, the three men were shoulder-deep in the sea.

"Looks as if we're going to get wet," Summer said.

"Are you a good swimmer?"

Summer glanced at the three men. They were out of her depth now and cutting through the water in champion style. But she had expected nothing less from SAS members. "Not that good. How about taking a quick dip, and we'll nab them when they tire of swimming."

"Sounds good to me."

Summer waded in and gasped. "Eek! It's colder than I thought."

Natasha scooped up a handful of water and flicked it at her. "Don't be a baby."

"Take that!" Summer retaliated with gusto then fled.

Natasha swam strongly after her and

seconds later, it was a full-on water fight. Summer laughed so hard she sank. A hand snaked around her waist, dragging her to the surface.

"Is this a private fight, ladies, or can anyone join?"

Louie and Jake stood nearby, which meant the arm around her waist belonged to Nikolai. Her pulse did a rapid cha-cha. She turned in his embrace, her bare legs brushing his strong thighs and immediately flames sprang to life, licking her with lust. She sucked in a hasty breath as she stared at him, recalling their kiss. The way his gaze drifted down to her lips told her he remembered too.

"Are you Summer's friends?" Natasha asked.

The curiosity in Natasha's voice made her spring away from Nikolai. She tried to stand and went under before he hauled her to the surface. She came up spluttering. "Ah." Heat grew in her cheeks and she rushed into speech. "This is Louie and Jake." She pointed to the two grinning men then gestured at the man holding her against his chest. "This is my neighbor, Nikolai."

"Hmm," Natasha said.

She packed a lot of meaning into that soft sound. The heat in Summer's cheeks soared to a new high, and she couldn't meet Natasha's gaze. "I think I'll go in now. I'm a bit cold."

Natasha tossed her head. "I'm going to swim out farther." She smiled at Jake and gave Louie the same treatment—a flash of white teeth and fluttering eyelashes. "Care for a race, boys?" Then she dived through a wave and raced off without waiting for an answer.

Louie and Jake took off with whoops and white water, leaving her and Nikolai alone.

Summer stared after them while every atom in her body sizzled, aware of his arm under her breasts, holding her afloat in the water. "You're meant to babysit me, not act as a guard dog."

"I'm the one who needs a keeper," Nikolai growled right next to her ear.

His breath feathered across her cheek, and she shivered, wanting nothing more than to turn in his arms, draw his head down and kiss him.

"Summer, don't."

"I'm not doing anything." His intense gaze made her stomach soar and swoop—the emotional person's version of an out-of-control roller coaster ride.

A wave rocked their bodies together. Her breasts flirted with his bare chest and she caught her breath at the lightning bolt of sensation. She glanced up and met the answering fire in Nikolai's eyes. Then, as she watched, his gaze iced over.

"We can't do this. You don't know me. The things I've done."

As he spoke, he loosened his grip on her arms and pushed her away.

"You don't know me, either. And you can't make decisions for me. Why won't anyone let me make my own mistakes?"

Much to her disgust, the end of her sentence came out on a wobble. Confrontation. She hated it, which was why she was running from the problem with her family. Deep down, she knew this truth. Sooner or later, her parents and brothers would learn she needed to live life on her own terms. Without babysitters. Her mother would cry.

Already, she felt the lash of guilt before uttering a word of her point of view.

"I promised Henry."

"Yeah, I know." Summer started for the shore and the splashing behind indicated he was getting out too. She waded through the water as if a stingray chased on her heels. She loved her parents and her brothers and knew they loved her, but they had to let her go. She just wished she could take her own advice and push away Nikolai.

Once she reached the sand, she paused. The strange thing though, was the way she consistently stuck up for herself with Nikolai. It felt good. Right. Maybe it was the enforced break from her family. "Will you walk with me along the beach?"

Caution chased surprise over his face. "All right." He fell into step.

"Do you have proof about Dare's family yet?"

"No, it's still rumor."

"Then please back off and stop following me. Dare's taken me to three different restaurants and today to the beach to meet his family. I haven't seen drugs or anything remotely illegal." Summer exhaled. "You realize that by playing the heavy-handed parent you're making me choose sides."

"I've noticed you're stubborn."

An inelegant snort escaped her. "Not usually. It's a new thing since I arrived in Auckland. Usually I let everyone ride roughshod over me."

On reaching the wooden wharf, they turned and ambled back to their starting point.

"So we agreed," she said, breaking the silence that had fallen between them.

"You'll trust me to look after myself without interfering? I promise to let you know if I have a problem. You'll go back to the original plan of watching from afar—getting a visual?" Her quick darting glance at him intercepted a fierce frown.

"I don't think that's—"

"You can't watch me twenty-four hours a day," she snapped. "You have to sleep sometime."

Chapter 7

Nikolai stared at Summer, taking in the stubborn jut of her chin, the flash in her blue eyes. Without thinking, he reached out to sweep a lock of damp blue hair off her cheek. Silky-smooth skin slid beneath his fingers, tempting him to explore. His gaze slid down, past her neck. Lingered.

He exhaled slowly, almost choking on the truth. He wanted her—in every possible way. He admitted it, despite fighting with every fiber of his being. Pity he couldn't introduce Summer to Laura, his ex. That would light a fire under her—all he'd see was dust once Laura listed his many faults as a husband, as a man. She'd never speak to him again.

"So, we're agreed?" she said, her voice low, strained.

Nikolai searched her countenance, saw the same physical awareness burning in her open gaze and groaned. Hell, who ever said life was fair?

"Look, if Henry were here, he'd tell you to give Martin the shove. I think you're playing with trouble, but I'll back off as long as you promise not to investigate Martin on your own. If you go out with him, make sure it's in a public place. Please, promise me that."

He kept the lie slick, as smooth as her soft skin, told it in an even tone and looked her in the eye the whole time. When she nodded, he felt like a pile of dog turds. Eventually, she'd discover his lie and would never look at him in the same way again.

The idea should've made him happy.

Summer stood on tiptoe and brushed a kiss across his cheek. "Thanks."

"Hey, Summer!" Natasha bounced up and down as she hailed them. Nikolai noticed his friends' sly amusement as they stood at the girl's side.

"Mum confirmed Dare's not coming back. Feel like going to the movies? Nikolai, you'll come with us? Jake and Louie said they'd like to go."

Nikolai waited for Summer to decide.

"Sure," she said. "Nikolai?"

"Sounds good, as long as we don't have to go to some weepy chick-flick."

After the movie, Nikolai gave her a ride home. In the dark, intimate confines of his car, she took the coward's route and pretended to sleep.

It wasn't that the evening hadn't gone well. It had. No, she was in full-out panic because during the movie, she'd discovered—admitted—she'd fallen for the man.

She huffed silently. Talk about a bolt from the heavens.

A clone of her brothers—a bossy take-charge male who liked to tell her what to do. And true to type, Nikolai had tried to veto her friendship with Dare, making him out to be second cousin to an ax murderer. Her fortitude strengthened as she recalled the past. She needed to use two hands to count the number of boyfriends her brothers had sent fleeing for cover.

The question was—what did she do now?

So far, independence meant fun, and she wasn't remotely tempted to give it up for something that might or might not be permanent. Maybe if she ignored the attraction and searched for another male—one who'd let her express her opinions and listen instead of reducing every word to clipped orders, someone other than Dare.

"Summer, are you awake?"

"Huh?"

"We're home."

She opened her eyes and straightened. So they were. Deep in thought she hadn't noted their progress. "Thanks for the ride home."

"I'll walk you to the door."

Despite her instinct to decline, she sucked in a deep breath and let it ease free. Pick your fights. "Thanks."

She scrambled from the car with her straw basket and rummaged for her house keys. They were right at the bottom, of course. Feeling the weight of his stare, she fumbled, and the keys dropped to the ground with a metallic rattle.

"Let me." He retrieved them and shoved the right key in the lock. "Hell, Summer. You didn't lock the door."

"Yes, I did. Don't you remember? You were spying."

"Stay there. Don't move." Then he slid through the open door into the darkness.

She ignored the order and followed cautiously.

"Don't you ever listen to what I say?" he demanded, materializing from the dark shadows on her right.

"When you ask instead of ordering, I might consider."

"There wasn't time to pretty it up."

"But—"

"Quiet." Nikolai shoved her behind him.

Summer heard a noise too. She snapped her mouth shut, freezing like the marble statue of Peter Pan in Uncle Henry's garden. The tenseness left him, and he dragged her close enough to whisper in her ear.

"Sounds as if they've gone out the window. You can come with me, but for God's sake, if I tell you to run, make sure you do. Can you do that?"

Astonishment made her blink, but she didn't let it show in her voice. "Yes. I understand." Her heart thudded as adrenaline morphed to higher levels, pressing against her instinct to run and hide.

"Come on then." Nikolai edged through the darkness, moving with stealth and confidence.

She attempted to emulate him, but

even though she was familiar with the surroundings, the lack of light threw off her judgment of distances. Not Nikolai. He never faltered.

In her uncle's den, he stopped abruptly. "They've gone. Turn on the light."

She flicked the switch and winced at the bright glare. The cords of the wooden Venetian blinds rattled against the sill, disturbed by the stiff southerly blowing in from the estuary. On closer observation, she noticed the muddy footprint on the sill.

She sighed. "Should I phone the police or check to see if anything is missing first?"

"I wouldn't worry too much about missing items."

The strange note in his voice made her jerk to attention. "Why not?"

He indicated the packets of white

powder sitting on the top of her uncle's desk.

"Are they what—?"

Sirens sounded in the distance, loud and insistent.

"Yep, I'd take that bet," he said, leaning against the wall. "Those packages aren't yours?"

Summer inched toward the desk, eyeing the items as if they might pounce. Curious, she reached out to touch.

"Don't." Nikolai moved so quickly she flinched. "You don't want to leave your fingerprints."

Her head thudded in sync with the advancing sirens. She stared wordlessly at Nikolai as a vehicle pulled up outside. The siren ceased and blessed quietness fell, not a sound except the drubbing of her heart and Nikolai's slow, controlled breathing.

A fist hammered on the door.

Nikolai dropped the arm from her shoulder. "I'll get it."

"No. Let me. You're not going to do anything stupid?"

"No point. The cops know it's here."

"How? I don't understand. This is a bad movie."

A bark of laughter sounded seconds before a fist pounded the door again. "Somehow, sweetheart, I think it's gonna get worse."

How? Her mother would have a cow if she heard, and the news would reach her family by bush telegraph. It always did. Masculine voices discussed forcing an entrance. "I'm coming." She yanked the door open before they took further action. "Yes?"

Blue and red lights flashed on top of the unmarked police vehicle. Two plain clothes cops stood on the doorstep, their identifications held aloft for her to inspect. She should've felt intimidated, but Nikolai's presence boosted her confidence. "Can I help you?"

"Police," one said unnecessarily.

"Can I do something to help you?" she repeated, standing in the middle of the doorway. "It is rather late."

"We've had a tip-off about one of our investigations. Can we come in?"

She scowled as the older of the two policemen advanced. She stood her ground. "Don't you need a warrant or something?"

Nikolai appeared behind her. "Let them in, Summer."

Wordlessly, she stepped back to allow the officers to enter.

"I think you'll find what you're looking for in the study," Nikolai said.

"Who are you?" the younger policeman asked.

"Nikolai Tarei." As he spoke, he moved closer and curved his arm around her waist, drawing her against his side. When she opened her mouth to speak, he tightened his grip, and she slammed her mouth shut. Inwardly, she fumed. Once again, he was taking charge.

"We have a few questions."

"Come through to the kitchen," Nikolai said.

Summer wanted to protest his highhandedness. She glared her annoyance, but he merely shook his head and propelled her into the kitchen. One of the policemen followed while the other stepped into her uncle's study.

"Can you tell us what this is about please?" she asked after subsiding into a chair. Her voice held clear impatience.

The policeman ignored her prompting. "Your name?"

"Summer Williams."

"Do you own this house, Mr. Tarei?"

"My uncle owns this house. Nikolai lives next door."

The second policeman entered the kitchen. He held the packets of white powder in his right hand. He wore gloves and held the packets by the corners.

"Do these belong to you, Miss Williams?"

"No."

"Do you have any idea how they came to be on the desk then?"

She glanced at Nikolai, and at his imperceptible nod, she answered the question. "Nikolai and I have been out all day. We returned fifteen minutes ago. The front door was unlocked, and when we came inside we both heard noises. By the time we investigated whoever was inside had left via the study window. If you look, you'll see a footprint on the windowsill."

"Hmm." The older policeman scratched the stubble on his chin. "I'd like you to accompany us to the station."

"I didn't expect them to keep us there all night," Summer muttered. "For a while there, I thought they were going to lock us up."

Nikolai shrugged as an unmarked blue sedan pulled up beside them. "This looks like our ride home."

He spoke to the driver and opened the back door for Summer. Nikolai slid in beside her and the car pulled away. On the short drive home, neither of them spoke.

"Looks like you have company, Summer."

Summer jerked upright, flushing at the realization she'd gone to sleep and used Nikolai as a pillow. Good grief. Had she dribbled on his shirt? She wiped her eyes with the back of her hands and surreptitiously checked her mouth and chin for dampness. "Sorry?"

"Martin's here."

Summer's head jerked up. She gasped, then turned back to stare at Nikolai. "What do I tell him?"

"I'd stick to the truth," Nikolai said in an undertone.

"At least I'll be able to prove he has nothing to do with crime."

"Maybe."

The car pulled up alongside Dare's convertible. After thanking the driver, they climbed out.

"Hi, Dare." Summer smiled. "Have you been waiting long?"

Dare's look held antagonism as he glared at Nikolai. She needed to get rid of Nikolai before things turned ugly.

"Thanks for the help, Nikolai. I'll see you later." She backed up her words with a wave, took Dare's arm and dragged him toward the front door. For once, Nikolai seemed to trust her to deal with the situation on her own.

"Where have you been?" Dare demanded in a low, furious voice.

Summer unlocked the door and stood back for him to enter. She refused to argue in front of Nikolai. She sensed his gaze even with her back to him. A tingle sprang to life inside her, and it had nothing to do with Dare's arrival.

She rubbed her gritty eyes and forced another smile. "I could do with a cup of coffee. Come through to the kitchen, and I'll explain everything. It's been a rough night."

Five minutes later, the scent of freshly ground coffee beans filled the air and coffee dripped into the carafe.

"You know Natasha and I went to the movies last night?"

"Yes."

"When Nikolai dropped me off here, someone was inside the house. Whoever it was left several packets of cocaine and called the cops to alert them."

"Cocaine?" Dare stared at her in astonishment.

The reaction was genuine. Summer would swear to it. "It wasn't good quality, but definitely cocaine. Lucky for me, the culprit left a boot print on the windowsill and none of the packets had my fingerprints on them, either inside or out. But the police still took me in for questioning. I've been there all night."

"The police don't have any idea who called them?" This time his voice held an edge, something off that made her wish she could read his mind. Men were so unpredictable.

She frowned at the coffeemaker and wished it would hurry. "No. They think the call was made on a cell phone—one of those prepaid ones that are difficult to trace."

"What was your next-door neighbor doing with you? Why didn't you call me?"

There had been a time, not long ago, when she would've felt thrilled to have two men pay attention to her. "I didn't call you because I thought you were busy."

"But you called him."

He sounded sulky. Male egos. She could do without them. "The police took him in for questioning too because he was still here."

"I don't like the way he hangs around or the way he looks at you. He probably called the cops."

Summer suppressed a snappish comeback. "He's my uncle's friend. I suspect my uncle asked him to watch out for me. I can't be rude. The coffee's ready. Black, isn't it?"

"Yeah." Dare paced the length of the kitchen. "Thanks," he added as an afterthought.

She plonked the mug on the wooden table and muttered under her breath when her undue force splashed coffee over the maroon tablecloth. She grabbed a rag to wipe up the spill and sat to savor her morning beverage.

Dare paused mid-pace and whirled to face her. His intense frown made her stare. As she watched, he strode past the table, past his waiting coffee. He was leaving? Or was he merely doing an extra large lap?

She swiveled in her chair. Her mouth dropped open when he kept going through the open door. "Dare, what about your coffee? Dare!"

"Something's come up. I have to go."

"Right now? Without drinking your coffee?"

"Sorry."

The apology lacked in sincerity, and she leapt to her feet. "What's come up?"

A flash of irritation flickered in him. His full mouth firmed as he checked his phone. "I need to go to work. A problem with a business competitor. I'll ring you later."

Talk about a pat on the head. She sank onto her chair. What had happened to make him run off that way? She replayed the last quarter of an hour in her mind and came up blank. One moment he'd been acting the jealous boyfriend, then the next he was in full business mode. Then, another thought occurred.

What if Nikolai was right about Dare? Did Dare know more than he was letting on about the drugs they'd found in Uncle Henry's study?

Chapter 8

Dare's abrupt defection niggled at her for the rest of the morning, so much so that she had difficulty concentrating on the Sunday paper. She half expected him to call yet heard nothing.

By two o'clock, she gave up waiting and grabbed the keys for her Mazda and her exercise gear. If she hurried, she could make the Tae Kwon Do class and shop for groceries on the way home. If Dare rang while she was out, too bad.

Her car started with the usual bad-tempered splutters, and she muttered and cursed before she and the car came to terms and traveled sedately toward Papakura. The traffic became heavier once she neared the motorway turnoff. People heading home after the weekend away. A flicker of loneliness brought a flash of homesickness for friends and family. She slowed at the intersection and indicated a right turn onto a quiet road that would get her to her class and avoid most of the traffic.

While she drove down the hedge-lined road, she puzzled over Dare's weird behavior. A screech of tires made her glance in her rear-vision mirror. Another vehicle was rapidly closing the distance between them.

She gulped when it kept coming, faster and faster.

Fear dried her mouth.

The reflection of a four-wheel drive vehicle filled her mirror—black with shiny silver chrome in the front. She pressed the accelerator. Tires shrieked and her aging car shuddered, protesting the demand for speed. The black monster continued to stalk her.

Every two seconds, like a magnet seeking metal, her gaze was drawn to her rear-vision mirror. A maniac. The driver was deranged.

She gripped the steering wheel, her heart galloping. If anything, he'd sped up.

"Idiot." Strong, colorful curses danced through her head. Her hands tightened on the wheel, while sweat broke out on her forehead, her palms—all over her body.

A witness. She needed a witness.

She prayed for a car to come from the other direction. It didn't happen. Instead, the roaring behind grew louder, more frightening. More threatening. She glanced in the mirror again and caught a glimpse of white teeth, lips curled in a wolfish smile.

A crash jolted her vehicle. Her car shot forward. Her body snapped toward the windscreen and jerked to a halt at the jam of the seat belt. Air exploded from her lungs, and she wheezed for replacement oxygen.

The four-wheel drive slammed into her bumper a second time. Metal ground against metal in a horrible, expensive grating.

Summer's car shunted off the road, flying over a low bank into a ditch. The branches of the roadside hedge scraped the window and the paintwork. Fingernails on a blackboard.

Her car plowed to a halt in the hedge, the branches blocking the sun. Her engine cut, and she heard the roar of the four-wheel drive as it slowed, the spray of gravel as it departed. Somewhere close, an animal bleated in fright, then all was quiet.

With trembling hands, she attempted to release her seat belt. A shaft of pain shot across her chest. A soft moan escaped. She had to get out of the car. What if it caught on fire? Or what if that idiot returned?

He'd rammed her car on purpose.

He'd wanted to frighten her.

To injure.

She reached for the seat belt release again and on her third try the button lowered, freeing the pressure on her breathing. A splash of blood dropped to her hand. She needed to... What did she need to do? It was nighttime, wasn't it? She'd go to sleep.

The plaintive moo of a cow jerked open her eyes. Somewhere in the distance, a dog barked. Summer blinked and realized she was in her car. That was right. She needed to get outside. She struggled with the door. It opened a fraction then slammed to a stop against something solid. The hedge shook, scraping against the car.

Jammed.

Try the passenger door. She reached for the handle, and an arrow of pain darted through her upper body while inside her head, someone played a drum solo. She gritted her teeth and kept pushing the door. Without warning, it dropped open. A blast of fresh air blew inside, caressing her hot cheeks.

Summer sucked in a painful breath and crawled from the driver's seat to the passenger side. The gear stick jabbed her thigh while the drum soloist worked into a crashing finale. She winced and wiped a hand across her cheek. It came away covered in blood.

Behind her, a vehicle pulled up. She froze, her heart leaping into her throat. The driver had returned. God, what was she going to do?

"You there! What the devil do you think you are doing? I heard you speeding. No wonder you drove off the road. Stupid idiot. Don't you watch the road safety ads on television? Probably been drinking," the masculine voice finished in disgust.

This didn't sound like the driver—not the way he was haranguing her. She crawled from the car and dropped into the long grass. Water seeped into her leggings while the stiff breeze tore at her hair. She shivered.

"You there! Are you all right?"

Was she all right? She considered the

question.

"Look at you." The man clicked his tongue in disgust, stomped closer, and when she lifted her head her vision filled with a pair of red-and-black gumboots. She tried to raise her gaze to his face but didn't get any farther than the patched knees of his faded woolen trousers before pain kicked her butt.

"If you've caused Mabel to go into premature labor, I'm gonna sue. Don't think I won't either, missy." The boots kept coming until they halted three inches from her nose, close enough to touch. "Huh! Should have known. You're one of those young punks with weird-colored hair and metal pins in places that I'm sure doesn't have the approval of the good Lord. You're bleeding." He tsk-tsked loudly. "Suppose I'll have to use that newfangled phone thing my daughter gave me for emergencies."

The man squatted beside her, his knees creaking. "Hope you know how to use this thing 'cause my memory is a bit hazy on the instructions. I'll ring for an ambulance, but I can't wait. I've got to check Mabel."

"I'm fine." Summer attempted to lift her head to survey the road for a body. She hadn't run over anyone. She hadn't. "Just ring Nik—" No! Not a good idea. She struggled to sit but ended in an undignified sprawl.

The elderly man pulled a cell phone from his pocket and eyed it doubtfully. He held it away from him then stabbed a button. A satisfied grunt emerged. After pushing more buttons and more grunting, he spoke. "Lisa, I need you to ring for an ambulance."

Summer heard a panicked squawk.

"Not for me, Lisa!" the man shouted. "Some fool girl has driven off the road. Right near Mabel's house. I don't know. Better ring the cops too. If Mabel's hurt, I want to sue."

The man shoved the phone back in his pocket, glanced at her then stood with another round of creaking joints. "Can you stand?" he demanded, his voice gruff.

Summer nodded and immediately wished she hadn't. The man with drums was still present in her head, her nod inducing him to pound louder. She bit her bottom lip and pushed upward. She made it to her feet but wavered, balance challenged. The man's hands shot out to steady her, strong and sure despite his age.

"Thanks," she mumbled, battling both

dizziness and the urge to throw up over the man's gumboots.

In the distance, the faint cry of sirens sounded.

"Good. They'll be here soon. Bleeding looks to have stopped. Lean against the car." The man led her to her Mazda. He glanced down the road, clear impatience showing in his lined face. He vibrated with worry.

Summer tried to focus. "I can't see...Mabel. Go check. She might need the ambulance."

The man's head whipped around to stare at her. "The vet maybe, but not the ambulance. Mabel is my angora goat."

A goat? A flash of yellow-and-green and the incessant screech of sirens told Summer help was at hand. Alice in Wonderland. All she needed was a pink rabbit to go with the goat, and she'd fit right in at the tea party. A mechanic... A tow company. She shuddered at the thought of repairs and the resulting bill. When would they turn off that infernal racket? Her right hand crept up to touch her throbbing temple.

"Over here," the old man hollered.

Summer moaned.

A lady in a white shirt and navy-blue trousers inserted herself in the gap between her and the elderly man. "Where does it hurt, love?"

"Head." Lord, did it hurt.

"What about your eyes? How many fingers am I holding up?"

She squinted through narrowed eyes. The fingers wavered, multiplying, changing from four to two and back again. In the end, she guessed. "Three?"

"Concussion," the woman murmured to a second man. "Come on, love. We'll get you to a hospital."

"But what about Mabel?" Summer demanded, her heart thudding with panic. She must have hit Mabel. That man had said so. "Is she hurt?"

"Was someone else in the car? Where are they?"

From behind her, a small cough sounded. The two ambulance attendees looked past her.

"Mabel is my goat," the man said. "Her house is the other side of the hedge. And if she's injured, I'm suing." His words were punctuated by a plaintive bleat.

Oh, yeah. A goat. Mabel was a goat. He'd told her that earlier. Thank goodness. She slumped, suddenly aware of every aching bone and muscle. A shiver danced through her as another mournful bleat sliced through her pounding head. She groaned. If her mother heard about this accident, she would yank every parental rein at her disposal. Summer would find herself back in Eketahuna quicker than Superman could change into his fancy duds.

The elderly man stomped into her range of vision. "Mabel doesn't sound good."

Perhaps this man was related to her mother?

"Sir, we need to get this woman to hospital. What's your name, love? Can we get the police to contact your family?"

"Summer." Funny, there were cartoon birds fluttering around inside her head. If she listened hard enough, she could hear their frantic tweeting.

"Summer, your family?"

The woman's last question finally registered. Family. No way. Nikolai's number. He'd help.

Nikolai.

Summer grimaced. Lately, she turned to him with all her problems. She was coming to rely on him. A sharp pain in her lungs reminded her to breathe. In fact, old Nikolai was like a handy-dandy crutch. Panic started to unfurl in her. Deep inside, it unraveled like a ball of her mother's yarn. Was she a person who needed a crutch?

The wail of another siren cut through the tentative chirp of birds and the buzz of a bee seeking nectar from the wildflowers. Mabel bleated indignantly on the other side of the hedge. A car pulled to a stop, sending a billow of dust sailing through the air.

Summer sneezed and held her aching head. At the sound of footsteps, she opened her eyes. Her gaze met with shiny black shoes and crisply pressed navy trousers.

"You," a masculine voice said. "We've just let you out of custody. How can you be in trouble again already?"

"She's a criminal. What did I tell you?" the elderly man cried triumphantly.

"You can talk to her later. We need to get her to hospital," the female attendant cut in.

Summer wanted to deny everything. All allegations. She was the innocent one here. Why did no one believe her?

The woman propelled her to the ambulance, and she subsided onto a soft mattress with a relieved sigh. Important things to worry about. Somehow, she possessed an enemy who was becoming bolder in their methods. She swam way out of her depth. Her journey to find herself and to assert independence had become fraught with problems. She required help. Nikolai.

Outside the ambulance, two policemen huddled together, talking in low voices. The one who interrogated her this morning stepped inside the ambulance.

"Someone rear-ended you."

She attempted to nod then groaned. "Yes," she gritted out past the swooping cartoon birds.

"Are you coming with us or staying here?" the female ambulance officer demanded.

"I'll stay. The evidence we've found changes everything. This accident looks deliberate." The detective stared at her, an assessing expression on his jaded, seen-it-all face. "Lady, you have an enemy, and he means business."

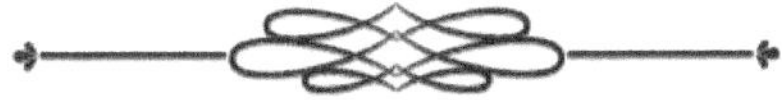

Nikolai eyed the lack of lights in the house next door for the third time in as many minutes. His gut churned as he checked his clock. Nine o'clock. Something was wrong. Every single one of his senses screamed it. The Mazda wasn't parked out front either.

That was even more alarming.

The throaty purr of a car drew his attention. The clotheshorse. Summer must be with him. Although he didn't want her spending time with the man, the tense set left his shoulders. His gut, however, continued to burn, and he reached for a tube of antacids.

Martin climbed out of his convertible and strolled to the front door. After a brisk knock, he stood back and waited expectantly. Nikolai hesitated, wondering whether to go out and interrogate the man or stay.

The continued uneasiness inside and his promise to Henry made the decision for him. That he'd begun to care about Summer in a sexual way, he shoved aside.

Nikolai slid out the open window and strode around to the front of Henry's house. He watched the man for a few seconds, hoping to pick up on the situation without the need of questions. When the man knocked a second time, he knew something had happened to Summer.

He stepped out of the shadows so Martin could see him. "Martin."

"You."

A smirk curled across Nikolai's lips. Like a dog sizing up the enemy, his grin widened to show teeth.

"Is Summer with you?"

Nikolai slouched against the trellis near the front door. Despite his relaxed posture, every muscle was primed to spring at the slightest hint of provocation. "I was gonna ask the same thing. I haven't talked to her since this morning."

"But she knew I was coming back. We were having dinner."

"Her car's gone." Nikolai straightened and stalked closer to Martin. The man appeared worried and that made Nikolai's insides burn with renewed vigor. "She left early afternoon."

Martin cursed under his breath. For a long drawn-out second they traded a stare.

Martin's face paled. The man knew something, and he was damn well going to share even if he had to beat it out of the man. Nikolai pounced, grabbing two fistfuls of linen shirt. "If something's happened to her because of you..." His glare concluded the sentence, and he took immense satisfaction in the way Martin inched away as far as he could, given Nikolai's grip on his person.

"Have you tried to ring her phone?" Martin asked.

Pique rippled through Nikolai. Hell, she hadn't given him the number. "Nope. Have you?"

"A couple of times. It rings but she doesn't answer. I've left a message, sent a text too, but she hasn't returned my call."

Nikolai released the man. "Give me your phone."

Martin stepped out of range before he dug in the rear pocket of his designer jeans. He pulled out a phone not much bigger than a cigarette packet. "Speed dial four."

Speed dial four. Why didn't the man just rub his face in it? Nikolai took the miniature phone and stabbed a button. He held the phone to his ear and prayed Summer would answer. Four rings. Five rings...

"Hello."

"Who is this?" Nikolai demanded. "Where's Summer?"

The person on the other end wasn't cooperative. "Who is this?"

"Nikolai Tarei. Summer's neighbor." Damn this man had better have answers.

"Detective Matthews."

Fear sliced through him with the suddenness of guerilla fire. "Where's Summer?" He listened to the detective, his grip tightening on the phone until white showed on his knuckles. "Yeah. Okay." He hit the end button and handed the phone back to Martin. "Summer's in the hospital. Someone rear-ended her vehicle and fled the scene." He didn't add that the detective had sounded worried even though the man had tried to hide it. Nikolai took a deep breath, but it did little to dispel his own rising fear.

"Hospital? What's she doing there?" Martin appeared uneasy, glancing at his watch every few minutes.

Nikolai wondered why. "Concussion concerns. They're keeping her in overnight. You coming to the hospital?" He hated to ask but Summer would want to see the man.

Dare checked his expensive wristwatch again. "I can't. I have an important meeting in half an hour. That's why I've been trying to ring Summer—to cancel our dinner date. Look, tell her I'm sorry. I'll check in on her later tonight."

"All right." Nikolai watched the man rush to his car, but instead of driving off, the man made a call. Weird. The clotheshorse wasn't acting as if he was in a hurry. He didn't seem worried about Summer either. If anything, he looked pissed.

Something or someone had rattled his cage.

Nikolai hurried inside to collect his car keys. The cushy babysitting number Henry had handed him was turning into the assignment from hell. Summer was in danger right up to her pretty little neck, and if he wasn't careful, he would go down with her.

Chapter 9

Nikolai stood at the door of the hospital room, his gaze on the still form in the narrow bed. His heart jumped and stuck halfway up his throat, his pulse hammering as if he'd just finished training maneuvers. She looked pale, so defenseless in the hospital bed, her blue-streaked hair a bright contrast to the wan face and the white pillowcase.

A cold sweat beaded his brow. Hell, if anything happened to her, he'd never forgive himself. This wasn't a mere job, a favor to Henry any longer. Somehow, somewhere along the line, she'd wormed into his affections with her smart mouth and sassiness.

He shook himself and stepped closer to the bed. He must've made a sound because her eyes popped open.

"Hi," she whispered.

"Are..." Nikolai paused to clear the lump from his throat. "Are you okay?"

She nodded but winced slightly, enough to let him know she needed to stay right where she was in the hospital.

He grabbed a chair from the adjacent cubicle and set it next to the bed. "Are you up to telling me what happened?"

"I was driving to my Tae Kwon Do class. The traffic was heavier than normal so I took one of the back roads. A vehicle raced up behind, rear-ended me on purpose and drove off."

"Bastard." Anger pumped through his veins. He didn't like the developing picture. Murky and disjointed as it was, it spelled danger. It was obvious someone wanted to hurt her, but that wasn't going to happen. His jaw tensed as he mentally prepared—even if he had to watch her 24/7.

The need to touch her, to reassure himself she was okay roared through him. After battling the urge for long tension-filled seconds, he gave in and ran his fingers across the smooth skin of her brow. It wasn't enough. He had a craving to haul her into his arms and hold her, body aligned to body.

A sexual charge jolted him, tightening his balls and jerking his cock. Instantly, disgust flew through his mind. She was hurt, yet he couldn't get past the sexual heat that licked through his veins whenever he was in the same room, breathing the same air as her. Hell, he wasn't sure whether to kiss her senseless or ream her out for her recklessness.

"I think it was on purpose. The second I went off the road, he slowed before fleeing."

Bastard.

Nikolai looked forward to punching his fist into the driver's gut as soon as he caught up with him. He had to get rid of the angst riding him somehow. "Did you get a good look at him?"

She sighed. "Not really. Not enough to pick him out from a group of people."

"Number plate?"

"It was covered with mud."

A nurse bustled into the room, her soft-soled shoes squeaking on the hard floor. "How are you feeling? Still have a headache?"

"Yeah." Summer sounded rueful, and Nikolai noticed she refrained from nodding this time.

"How long before she can go home?"

"Tomorrow morning," the nurse answered with a cheerful grin. "Keeping her overnight is a precaution. Your wife will be fine, Mr. Williams."

"Thank you." Nikolai caught Summer's hand and laced their fingers together, ignoring the soft choked sound that emerged from her.

"There was a phone call at the desk for you earlier. Your brother. He said he'll be by later to visit," the nurse said.

Summer's hand tightened within his, and her mouth opened to deny the possibility. Nikolai sent her a silent warning with an imperceptible shake of his head.

"Thanks," he said to the nurse. He waited until the squeak of her shoes faded before he voiced his suspicions. "Did you get someone to contact your family?"

"No. I asked the detective to ring you."

"It took him long enough."

"He apologized for the delay. Your cell phone was switched off, and then he was called out on another case and forgot. He was embarrassed. And I couldn't ring anyone because my phone was in the car. The detective found it. Like I said—embarrassed. I think that's why he made a special trip to drop it off. Anyhow, I didn't ask him to ring my family. If they get wind of me being in the hospital, they'll arrive en masse and ship me back to Eketahuna before I have time to blink." She clutched his arm with a hint of desperation in her blue eyes. "Please don't contact them. You heard what the nurse said. I'm all right."

"If that wasn't one of your brothers on the phone, then we have a problem."

Nikolai thought rapidly and came up with one solution. He needed to take her home, but first he'd check with the medical staff.

He stood. "I'm going to find a doctor. If anyone comes in here and you think they're suspicious, press on the call button. Don't let up until someone answers. I'll be back as soon as I can."

He returned in under ten minutes, his gut twisting with uneasiness the entire time he was away from her. When he strode back into the hospital room, he found Summer asleep, her hand clutched around the call button. He considered telling her the clotheshorse intended to drop by to see her but decided to ignore his conscience. He'd keep her away from the man until he knew what was going on and where the danger lurked.

Her eyelids flickered. "Nikolai?"

"Yeah, sweetheart. Come on, let's get you dressed, and we'll split this joint."

"We're going?" She sounded fractionally more alert.

"Yeah. Under the circumstances, the doctor said I can take you home." He tugged away the thin sheet and helped her stand. No point filling her in on the rest of their conversation.

"Stay in the front," she mumbled.

Her disgruntled tone brought a grin. "Scared?"

"Cautious." She wobbled a little.

Nikolai held her firm. "I'll close my eyes." Not that he meant a word. He was a red-blooded male. Of course, he'd peek if she gave him the opportunity.

She wavered again, and he took control. He deftly undid the tapes that laced the hospital gown at the back and tugged it down her arms. She wore high-cut, pale blue panties beneath and nothing else. Nikolai paused, his gaze on her luscious breasts.

"You're beautiful," he murmured with a trace of awe. Coral-colored nipples were puckered, as if begging for his touch. He swallowed before recalling the need for urgency. They needed to leave before Summer's so-called brother turned up.

Wordlessly, he held out a T-shirt for her. Once she was safely covered, he handed her the pair of leggings and steadied her while she dressed.

Nikolai shrugged out of his leather jacket and handed it to her. "It's cold out," he said at her hesitation. Once she donned the jacket, he curled his arm around her waist, and they walked from the room.

Despite the need to get her home and

into bed, Nikolai took the precaution of driving in a roundabout route to make sure they didn't pick up any followers. Thirty minutes later, he drove into his garage and lowered the door using his remote control.

By the time he carried a sleeping Summer inside, stripped her to the sexy panties and placed her in his bed, all hints of temper had dispersed, leaving outright fear. Her reckless behavior of jumping before she considered the consequences had landed her hip-deep in trouble. If he wasn't careful, it would get her killed.

Nikolai brushed tendrils of blue-streaked hair from her face. His gut twisted with tenderness at her childlike innocence while an ironic smile curled his lips. He couldn't wait to see the expression on her face when she woke to find him in the same bed. Difficult to guess her reaction. It could be outright horror or it could be...

His body tightened enough that he didn't have to second-guess his thoughts. He was bloody sick of fighting the sexual thing hovering between them.

Gritting his teeth, he ripped a black T-shirt over his head. He couldn't afford to relax his guard even if he gave into the lure of the woman. Summer was his responsibility and this time he intended to prove his competence, despite the fact he'd never asked for the job in the first place.

His hands went to the button closure on his jeans. He hesitated, shrugged and removed them, tossing the denims on the floor. She wanted grown-up. This adult male slept naked and since she was the guest, she'd have to abide by house rules.

He snorted at that piece of brilliance. Hell, and he thought she pushed the boundaries. Seemed he was ready to do some shoving of his own.

Summer woke cocooned in warmth and sublime comfort, apart from something digging into her back. Half awake, she stretched and tried to wriggle away from the object. A masculine groan froze her mid-wriggle. Her heart leapt while her brain processed the available information.

Warm. Male. Hard object.

Holy heck! She hadn't. She didn't.

Who?

She scrambled from the warmth, clutching the sheet to her naked breasts.

"You awake?" Nikolai asked, his voice low and gritty.

He looked sleepy, sexy and dangerous as hell to every single one of her resolutions to stay away from men of her brothers' ilk.

Yep, temptation personified.

She eased farther away even as her gaze traced the dark stubble on his jaw and slid lower to take in his broad shoulders. Naked shoulders. She searched for answers and came up empty.

Just her luck. She'd managed to corral a sexy man, there wasn't a parent or brother in sight, and she remembered zilch about the experience.

Zilch. Zip. Nada.

"Are you okay?" Nikolai propped himself up on his elbow and scrutinized her face.

A surge of heat collected in her cheeks. Inwardly, she tested her body. Nothing ached. Nothing hurt. She still wore her panties, but that didn't necessarily mean anything. She didn't feel the slightest difference. She should feel something.

Shouldn't she?

"Did we…ah…do anything I should know about?"

Nikolai's eyes narrowed then a slow grin spread across his lips. "Was it good for you too, sweetheart?"

"Don't you know?"

The grin transformed into a full-out chuckle. "Nothing happened."

The surge of disappointment wasn't unexpected, but hiding it…

She averted her gaze from his humor-filled face, chagrined by his lack of action. She had a man in the same bed, and he couldn't bear to touch her.

"Not yet."

The husky tone drew her back, but it was the seductive grin that held her still.

"Not...not yet?" Her words were scarcely louder than a whisper, and they seemed to hang in the air.

His gaze dropped to her breasts. "I thought we might explore a few possibilities."

Summer's jaw dropped. "Possibilities?"

"Is there an echo in here?"

"You're not making any sense. I'm confused."

"That makes two of us," he muttered and pounced.

She found herself flat on her back, staring up at him. "What are you doing?"

"I don't know." His grin was slow and very personal. "If I find out, I'll let you know."

"Reassuring," she whispered. The hot

look in his dark eyes made her breasts throb unbearably.

He combed his fingers through her hair, gently removing snarls from her curls. "Do you have a headache?"

"No. Is that my way out?" Her heart beat so fast she was sure he'd notice. The sweet ache in her breasts intensified, and she writhed uneasily, curious and yet nervous.

Nikolai traced the shape of her mouth with his forefinger. "That mouth of yours is full of sass. One day it's going to get you in trouble." He dipped his head and replaced his finger with his mouth.

Summer huffed, feeling as if someone had yanked the ground from beneath her feet. But not Nikolai. He took total control, angling and aligning their mouths for deeper contact. She clutched his shoulders and let him kiss her, part of her surprised and astonished by the reality.

Nikolai was kissing her of his own free will. What was wrong with this picture?

He lifted his head and smoothed the back of his hand across one cheek. "What's wrong?"

"I'm not sure. You tell me."

"You're looking confused."

She frowned. Although she found Nikolai attractive—very attractive—she wasn't sure the idea of them together was a good thing. In some cases, one plus one didn't equal two. She sucked in a deep breath and met his gaze without hesitation. "That's because I'm feeling confused. What's happened to change your mind?"

He toyed with one of her blue curls. The man seemed fascinated by her hair. "Someone is after you. You could have died yesterday."

Yesterday seemed hazy. Dreamlike. "Oh, yeah. The goat."

"The scum ball who ran you off the road," he said in a hard voice. "It made me realize we're wasting time. We want each other. We should act on it."

She darted a gaze past his right shoulder then shifted her attention back to him. "Who are you, masked man? What have you done with the big, bad SAS man?"

"He's still here, and he's fed up with talk."

"Oh, an action man," she purred.

Nikolai bent to kiss her again, his hands gliding beneath the sheet covering her partial nakedness. "I could always put you over my knee."

A quiver rocked her. "I must be sick. That actually sounds like fun."

He drew in a sharp breath. "Enough." He took her lips in a masterful kiss that left her in no doubt of his impatience with talk. The sheet disappeared from between them and without warning, skin touched skin.

She forgot about talk, her mind on his bare chest flattening her breasts. He traced the shape of her lips with his tongue and teased them apart. Her pulse danced in an erratic beat. Her hands curled around his upper arms, her fingers flexing against his biceps. She made a shy foray with her tongue, probing the cavern of his mouth, learning his taste and texture.

Nikolai pulled away to study her. "I shouldn't be doing this, but so help me, I don't think I can stop." His voice was low, smoky and a trifle unsure, but his eyes blazed full of passion.

"I want this, Nikolai. I'm not a child. I know what I'm doing."

"Glad one of us does."

If he started spouting about their age differences...well, murder looked enticing. She thought frantically and came up with one possible solution. Not her best but it might work. She pushed his shoulders until he moved off her.

He flopped over on his back and stared at the ceiling. "You don't have to shove—"

She launched across the bed and pinned him in place. "Don't move an inch."

For an instant he appeared nonplussed, then a sexy grin sprang to life, making his eyes twinkle with pure devilment. "Sweetheart, I'm all yours. Do your worst."

A snort tickled her throat. Now why

didn't she believe that? The man couldn't help himself. He'd take control at some stage. Her lids lowered to hide the burst of excited emotion that tore through her body.

She might not have experience with sex, but she wasn't a librarian for nothing. She, Summer Williams, was hell on wheels when it came to research and intended to put every bit of her knowledge to use.

Sucking in a breath, her gut and all other necessary parts, she stood and rounded the bed. He followed her progress, his avid scrutiny on her breasts, her waist and hips. Everywhere his gaze touched, her skin tingled.

A light-headed sensation flooded her mind—part fear, part exhilaration—sort of how she imagined a person felt while standing on the edge of a bungee platform. If she added hunger to the pot, along with curiosity and good old-fashioned lust, then she had the makings of a successful affair.

She stooped close, giving him a good view of her breasts. The sharp intake of his breath gave her confidence a boost. There were two people in this game. At the same time as she flashed her boobs, she tugged the cotton sheet covering him. Feeling like a kid at Christmastime, she peeled it back and excitement flooded her, drying her mouth as inch by inch she revealed his body.

She mentally added tight abs, muscled and strong, plus slim hips to the set of broad shoulders and the spectacular almost hairless chest. The sheet snagged at this point, and a renewed surge of heat flooded her features. Somehow, seeing a male penis in books was different from viewing the real thing.

A soft choking noise dragged her gaze from the tented sheet at his groin to the glint in his eyes. His mouth twitched as though he was trying to choke back a laugh.

"Your wish is my command, sweetheart."

She'd have to be both blind and deaf to miss the overt challenge. Your wish is my command. Huh! She forced a sly smile to her mouth even though the effort brought another flood of mortification to her skin. Then, recalling an article from Miranda magazine, she let her tongue snake out to lick her lips, while making sure he had an excellent view of her performance.

To her immense satisfaction, his laughter vanished, replaced by alertness. His hands clenched beneath his head, his features tightened and even better, a tic throbbed to life at his jaw.

Right, now she had his attention, she'd continue her exploration. Her pulse rate did a bump and grind as her attention returned to the tented sheet at his groin. As she watched, it twitched. A soft groan from the other end of the bed fueled her courage, but even so, her hand trembled as she lifted the covering from his lower body.

The man was all muscle and tanned skin, but it was his...his cock, she thought, determined not to act old-maidish at the first hurdle. Long and thick, it jutted out and upward. Nikolai watched her, no doubt waiting for her to bolt.

That wasn't going to happen.

She wanted to touch him so badly her breasts tingled, the tips tight and achy while her panties had grown damp. She planted her butt on the edge of the bed, right next to his hipbone. The position was awkward, so she crawled onto the mattress and wantonly straddled his legs.

Under her fascinated gaze, his cock jerked and seemed to grow even larger. Longer. As if hypnotized, she reached out to caress the warm length of him. Her palm curled around his shaft as she explored. Warm—yes. Smooth yet with an underlying strength. The cliché of satin over steel fit perfectly, and she could see why the expression was used so often in romances. Not exactly attractive to the eye but fascinating.

She ran her thumb along the length of him and caressed the smooth, swollen head. A deep red, almost purple color with a tiny slit at the end. As she smoothed her thumb across the slit, a bead of liquid appeared. She collected the glistening drop with a finger, and Nikolai jerked, a low moan issuing from deep in his throat.

Okay, so she hadn't killed him. Yet.

She absently worked her hand along his erection while she pondered what to do next. An article in Miranda magazine popped into her mind. Oral sex. The thought didn't horrify her—in fact, it sounded interesting. She bent closer and stroked her tongue down his shaft to the base. He groaned, and the twitch of his hips made her smile.

Power.

She had the ability to bring the soldier to his knees. She repeated the move, breathing deeply. He smelled faintly of soap and tasted a little salty. Musky. She licked around the swollen head and lapped across the slit. Another bead of liquid appeared, and she cleaned it away. Then she opened her mouth and took the tip of his erection inside, swirling her tongue around him as if he were an ice cream.

"Summer," he whispered hoarsely.

Using one hand, she scraped her hair back from her face and glanced up at him. The deep emotion in his eyes sent her pulse skittering. The knowledge she was responsible for his expression made the small victory even sweeter. She lapped around the head of his cock again, loving the taste and the sounds he made. His hips jerked, pushing him deeper into her mouth before he drew away.

She stared in surprise. He'd seemed

to enjoy her attention. Why was he stopping? "Why?"

"Not for your first time. It is your first time?"

She nodded, unable to take her eyes from his face, his mouth. She felt as though she balanced on a tightrope with the object of her desire inches away. A sweet ache pulsed in her lower belly, the harbinger of more to come.

"I should be shot." Nikolai brushed his hands over his face before centering his attention on her. "I want your pleasure too. Not just mine."

Summer licked suddenly dry lips. Had she been too forward? Too eager? "So, what do you want to do?"

"Let's start with lovemaking beginner's level." A gentle smile took the sting from his words. "The first thing we should do is even the odds. I'm feeling underdressed." His eyes focused on the silky blue fabric screening her from his sight. "What do you say?"

His words wound around her heart and gripped so tightly she could barely think let alone answer. Her hands skimmed down to her hips, and she pushed her fingers under the elastic band.

"Let me." He charged into action before she could think, let alone voice the reasons why showing her naked body in broad daylight was bad. He tugged the panties down her legs. Seconds later, she found herself flat on her back with Nikolai looming over her. Gone was the sullen soldier who looked after her under protest. Gone was the teasing male who'd suggested they start with the basics.

"You're so beautiful," he said in a low voice she had to strain to hear. "I don't know why you picked me, but I'm not giving you another chance to get away."

"I don't want to get away. I want...you."

He stroked one of his hands the length of her body, from her collarbone, over one quivering breast and lower, across her belly to come to a stop at neatly trimmed, heart-shaped pubic hair. He glanced up. "Now this is a surprise." His head dipped and he ran his tongue around the small heart.

Summer felt his touch clear to her toes. The throb in her belly centralized, and she stirred restlessly, needing his touch. Heck, she'd start begging soon, and from the glint in his eyes, the man knew it.

"I touched you," she pointed out, not happy with the breathy sound of her voice.

"Yes." He splayed her legs and settled between them, his gaze on her nether regions.

She gulped. Her pussy. Instantly, the heat intensified there. To her mortification, liquid bloomed. She squeezed her eyes shut.

Masturbation had never, ever made her this hot. Already, she felt as if she'd burst from her skin, and he'd scarcely touched her. Damn, she might beg yet.

"So pretty." His fingers traced around her heart then drifted lower still to her aching center. He brushed his thumb over her clit, just enough to give her a buzz. The sensation that shot through her was half pleasure, half pain.

"More. Harder. I need you to touch me." The words rushed past her lips, and she waited for a smug male act.

It didn't happen.

Nikolai smoothed his thumb across her clit again and pushed one finger into her tight channel. His finger eased the emptiness inside her, pushing it to something more.

"That would feel so much better if it was you."

"Last time I checked, the finger belonged to me."

Cursed color filled her cheeks, but she battled onward to complete her thought. "I mean you. Your cock," she added with a trace of defiance.

He gave a bark of laughter. "Still trying to run this campaign, sweetheart? This is my turn. We'll do things my way." He slid a second finger inside her, pushing them deep.

She quivered at the sense of fullness and concentrated on every sensation. The shimmer that swept her body with each cruise of a finger across her clit. The thud of her heart. But most of all, she savored the feeling of closeness, of sharing something intensely personal with Nikolai.

A different sensation across her clit made her eyes fly open. Nikolai's head was bent as he tongued her clit, teasing the small nub until pleasure roared through her, and she balanced on a pinnacle. His fingers slowly pumped in and out while he continued to tease. She lifted her hips, trying to maintain pressure on her aching clit. The feeling was too much. It wasn't enough.

She wanted...she wanted...

Nikolai met her gaze. He licked around her clit, the bundles of nerves jumping while he maintained eye contact. She couldn't have looked away if she tried. His pupils were huge. Black. Full of heat and promise.

With each pass of his tongue, she

throbbed with increased sensation. He picked up the pace, alternately licking her clit and filling her with his fingers.

The ache intensified until it became painful. Each lap of his tongue made it worse. Made it better. She swallowed and bit her bottom lip, trying not to cry out. Making love felt so much better with Nikolai. So much better. More fulfilling than self-pleasuring.

Another slow foray of his tongue deepened her excitement. Her lower body prickled and throbbed. Her hips lifted sharply upward, but he grasped one hipbone, holding her still. One soft drag of his tongue across her sensitized clitoris sent her over the edge. She shuddered deeply, her clit pulsing, sending spasms of pure pleasure shooting the length of her body. Her pussy clasped his fingers, gripping him in rhythmic bliss.

Slowly, slowly she floated back into her body, dazed at the experience.

Nikolai moved up the bed to kiss her. She tasted herself on his breath and something else that was uniquely him—wild, and dangerous and intense. Their tongues twirled in a lazy dance before he pulled away. He fingered a nipple, and automatically she arched her back, moving into his caress.

"You're so responsive to my touch. Beautiful." He rained a trail of kisses from the corner of her mouth, down her neck and across her collarbone. When his mouth latched on to a nipple, a prickle of renewed heat slid through her veins. The tug of his mouth caused a corresponding pull, a clench of her womb.

She clasped his head to her breast, her

fingers tangling in his black hair. "That feels wonderful. I want more."

He pulled away, releasing her nipple to gaze up at her with slumberous eyes. "There's more yet," he promised. "And it will be even better."

Her heart flip-flopped, and she couldn't help the blazing smile of approval that curved her lips. "More?"

"Oh, yeah." He tugged a lock of her hair, the small pain making her frown. Smiling, he covered her mouth with his, feeding from her lips and stoking the fire inside her to greater heights.

Nikolai cupped a breast and tucked a hand under her butt, aligning their bodies together. His penis fit between her legs, fueling longing in her.

"I want you so bad, but it's not too late to change your mind."

"Too much talk. More action required."

Nikolai clutched her against his larger frame, squeezing the air from her lungs. "Don't say I never gave you the opportunity," he said in a fierce tone.

He left her then, leaving her gazing at him in bewilderment, but when he opened the top drawer of his bedside table, enlightenment followed in the guise of a small foil packet.

She gulped in dismay. The articles in Miranda magazine stressed protection, but in the heat of the moment the advice had slipped her mind. Not Nikolai. He ripped the foil packet open with his teeth.

"Can I do it? Put the condom on for you?"

"Not this time, sweetheart. I'm too close. One touch and I'll lose it."
He smoothed the rubber on with an expertise she admired. "I'd rather come

inside you."

Oh, boy. Grown-up stuff. She wanted that too.

He trailed a hand across her belly and journeyed downward to circle her clit. A frown crossed his face, and he glanced up at her. "This might hurt. Talk to me. Tell me what you're feeling."

Real grown-up stuff.

His nimble fingers skated across her clit, parted her folds and pressed into her channel.

"It turns me on knowing you're wet for me, that you want me so much." His large frame shuddered as he uttered the words, and he pulled his finger from her, replacing it with the blunt tip of his cock. He trembled again. "I'll take this slow, even if it kills me."

Her breath caught as he pushed inside her, stretching untried muscles until she felt unpleasantly full. At her wince, he withdrew. Panicked, she clutched his tight buttocks, only relaxing when he pushed into her again, a little farther this time.

"You're tight," he murmured, surging and retreating, pushing deeper still.

A twinge of pain took her by surprise. A cry escaped, and he stilled, seated deep inside her. The sense of fullness was weird, yet she liked it once the pain receded. He kissed her, and after searching her face, continued with his strokes and kisses. His tongue plunged into her mouth with the same slow pace as his cock. Each easy stroke of his cock massaged her clit.

Soon she picked up the rhythm, moving with him in countermoves. Her delight in the act, the wisps of pleasure grew. Gradually, he increased his speed, cupping a butt cheek in each hand to lift her higher and angle his strokes.

She felt the familiar hum of arousal streak from her clit. She groaned and swallowed, directing his strokes with an insistent grip on his backside. She was close. So close.

"Nikolai," she breathed, reaching, searching for more. Suddenly she was there. Heat scorched her body, streaking along her length. Ripples of fulfillment shot through her body for long seconds after. It was like a signal to Nikolai. He stroked harder, faster. Quicker. Her pussy clenched around his cock with never-ending ripples.

He groaned, his hips thrusting in quick, frantic strokes, then he stilled.

When his breathing returned to something resembling normal, he eased from her body. Before she could speak, he folded her into his arms as if she were the most precious object.

Nikolai held her, running his hands across her sweaty back, his body heat searing her chest, making her feel safe, and valued. Making her feel loved.

Making her hope for the future.

Chapter 10

Nikolai held Summer, savoring the feel of her plastered against his body. He couldn't regret making love to her, even though he knew Henry wouldn't see things the same way. He didn't look forward to meeting her family or reacquainting himself with her brothers. Good blokes to have on the same side in a war, he knew from a previous mission when his team had combined with their unit. The two Williams brothers were an unstoppable force. He shrugged, knowing he wouldn't change things even if he could. The only way to keep Summer safe was to remain at her side.

"Whatz the time?"

"Just gone eight."

Summer bounded upright and almost fell off the bed. "I'm going to be late for work. Mrs. Ferguson will have a cow."

"You're not going to work today," Nikolai said.

"But I—"

"I'll ring Mrs. Ferguson. What's the number?" He climbed from the bed and grabbed his jeans off the floor. Seconds later he held up a cell phone, his finger poised to dial.

"This will be good. Does it have speaker phone? I can't wait to hear Mrs. Ferguson get the better of you."

Nikolai loved the way Summer said what she thought and stood up to him. Laura had acted frightened, watching him as if he were a lit fuse. A throwback to her childhood, he presumed, since he'd never hit a woman in his life. He hadn't realized how much Laura's quiet anxiety had bugged him until he'd come face-to-face with Summer's feistiness.

"You'll have to listen to a one-sided conversation." Someone picked up the phone on the other end and he asked for Mrs. Ferguson. A minute later, he hung up. "There. What did I tell you?" He smirked when she rolled her eyes.

Nikolai glanced at the clock again and aimed for casual as he sat on the bed beside her, or as nonchalant as a man could be with a raging hard-on. "We have time for breakfast or to sleep longer. Your call."

Dark brows shot upward, and her breasts jiggled at her abrupt shoulder shrug. He would've been half dead if he hadn't appreciated the sight.

"Would there be sleep involved?" she asked in a throaty drawl.

"That would depend on you." He felt humor flirt with his lips, although he tried to keep it low-key and under control. He didn't want to frighten her off, but hoped like hell she wanted a repeat performance as much as he did.

Summer pursed her lips, but he caught the twinkle in her blue eyes. "Actually, I have a few ideas."

"Yeah?" The naughty sparkle hiked his pulse rate, made his imagination race. This was the woman who'd been a virgin. Call him a macho pig, but he was meant to be the one leading the way. The wry thought had his head shaking. Luckily, he hadn't verbalized that one. Summer had already objected about her allocation to the little woman slot.

"We should try some different positions. For a start."

Nikolai found himself shocked, mouth

gaping momentarily. Hell, he'd created a sex monster. "Sounds interesting," he said cautiously. "What did you have in mind?"

"Everything," she said simply. "Anything you want to teach me."

Nikolai scanned her earnest countenance. Everything covered an awful lot of ground. He closed the distance between them. "Are you sure you feel okay? No headache?"

"I'm more than all right." She leaned against a pillow and stretched her muscles like a cat.

Unlike some women he'd been with, she didn't seem self-conscious displaying her body. She wasn't cowering under the sheet, moaning about big hips, the wrong size breasts, or a large butt. A refreshing change.

"Why are you grinning?" she

demanded, her lips curving in a sultry pout. The mischievous glint remained. "Going through your repertoire of positions?"

A snort escaped. Positions. What would she come out with next?

He advanced on her, intending to crowd her, to make her aware of him. And to fill her mind so full of him, she wouldn't keep trying to control proceedings. Off-balance worked for him.

"What do you know about positions?"

"I'm a librarian. I'm good at research. There's missionary, which we've done, doggy-style, ride—"

Nikolai lowered his head. Only one surefire way of shutting her up. His lips closed over hers just as she let loose a giggle. It was like kissing a glass of champagne. He'd never particularly liked the girly drink. On Summer, it tasted classy and made him hotter than he'd ever experienced before. Their lips slid together, tasting, sipping until the laughter disappeared and sexual energy arced between them.

Amazing. Bloody amazing.

He let his tongue flicker into her mouth to explore the moist warmth beyond. His cock ached for action. God, he wanted to sink into her warmth any way he could. Like a Neanderthal, he just wanted to fuck her. Immediate satisfaction.

He parted their lips to kiss a trail down her neck, exploring the curve of her chin, the delicate skin behind her ear where a pulse beat madly. He scraped his teeth lightly over the jumping tic, and she moaned.

"That feels amazing," she murmured. "I have the urge to tell you to bite harder, to mark me." Summer lifted her head then, full of sultry promise that pushed his heartbeat into a gallop. "Except Mrs. Ferguson does neck check every Monday morning."

"I thought you worked in a library?"

"Yeah. Mrs. Ferguson is big into leading by example. Hickeys don't set a good example to our younger customers. Hickeys are directly responsible for teenage pregnancy."

Pregnancy. For one frozen millisecond, Nikolai pictured her swollen with his child. And once the idea took root, it was difficult to shake. He expelled a breath and brutally pushed aside the vision. He'd been a father once, and a damn fine job he'd made of that. Soldiers had no right thinking about parenthood if they couldn't be home to raise their children and keep them safe. Last time he looked, he was still in the military. Same problem.

A soft touch on his cheek jerked him back.

"Where were you?"

"Just trying to decide which position."

"Go on. Don't keep me in suspense."

A bark of laughter escaped him as he grabbed Summer and rolled her on top of him. "We'll start slow with you on top."

"I always liked riding."

Her cheeky grin brought awe to the surface. She made everything fun, and it was a new experience for him. Almost as though he were the pupil and she the teacher.

"Come up here." Perhaps it was time to enjoy the fun, embrace it. He patted the bed at chest level. "So I can see better."

"That's not the business end," Summer retorted, not moving an inch.

"I'm the teacher here." His mouth quirked. Man, she cracked him up. "Why don't you follow instructions like a good soldier?"

"I don't do orders."

"No, but aren't you curious?" Of course, she was. The inquisitive spark flaring in her eyes glowed true and clear. "Come up here. Please."

Summer moved at the pace of a geriatric snail. Intense anticipation roared through him while he waited. The urgent need to claim her pulsed through his mind, but he wanted to prolong the loving, and make it mind-blowing for both of them.

"Stop there." His voice emerged hoarse and tight. Summer still straddled him and, stretched as she was, she gave him the perfect view. Her dark pubic hair was trimmed into the sexy heart while the rest of her was smooth under his questing gaze. "You're pretty. Plump and ripe for my touch." As he spoke, he strummed a finger across her labia and parted the folds. Using his hands, he urged her closer and blew softly on her swollen clitoris.

Summer swayed. A small mew escaped. Nikolai glanced up, enjoying the sight of her ripe breasts and pillowy curves. He blew again, and her body jerked. So responsive. He drew one finger the length of her swollen flesh, ending with a slow circle around her nub. Her juices moistened his finger as he repeated the process.

"Touch me," she pleaded in a breathless voice. "No teasing."

Nikolai smiled. Teasing was half the fun with a woman as hot as Summer. "Tell me what you want. Be precise so I don't get it wrong."

She sucked in a harsh breath. Her lovely breasts lifted then settled, her nipples tight and needy, reminding him he had to explore her a little more.

"Okay." She sounded breathless but determined. "I want you to touch my clit with your tongue. I want you to lick me until I'm hot and can't bear it anymore. Then I want you to put your cock inside me. I want you to thrust hard and fast while I ride you. I want you to make me come."

Proud amusement replaced the niggling doubt inside him. He'd been right. Nothing fazed her. She wasn't all talk about wanting to meet on equal terms. She wanted a man who challenged her and could accept any challenges she issued. Nikolai felt his balls tighten painfully. He hoped he could keep up with her demands.

"Is that all?"

"For starters," she said primly.

"You got all that from research?" He brushed his thumb across her clit, reveling in her sigh, her musky scent.

"Yeah."

Man, he couldn't wait to hear what else she had in mind. "Move a little closer." He positioned her level with his mouth and breathed deep. She smelled of sex and citrus and tasted better. Going slow and easy, he parted her folds and raked his tongue along her cleft, then teased her clit with a much lighter pressure. She shuddered and issued a soft moan that tugged at his cock. He felt his dick lengthen while the air crackled with sensual tension.

Nikolai listened to his body and increased the pace. Instead of teasing, he licked and tasted her engorged flesh. Summer was so wet for him, and a vocal lover.

"More. Harder. I need you inside me."

Nikolai gave her the steady thrust of his finger while he continued to lap and nibble around the edge of her clit, feeding on her juices, and urging her higher and higher.

"Oh, Nikolai. I'm so close. Stop. It's too much."

He didn't think she meant that so he kept pushing her higher, thrusting two and then three fingers deep inside her while he licked and sucked some more, slowing now to tease because he loved the way she moaned, her hips gyrating, silently pleading for a deeper possession.

"No more!" Summer wrenched away, her chest rising and falling rapidly as if she'd exerted herself. She ran a hand the length of his cock, her thumb smoothing across the drop of pre-cum at the end. "I want to come with you inside me. I want to feel your cock stretching me."

"Condom," Nikolai said. Damn, she unmanned him with her honesty. His gaze wandered the curves of her rounded backside as she bent to retrieve a foil packet from his bedside cabinet. Tempted, he ran his hand across one smooth butt cheek and down the crack between, down her perineum until his fingers skimmed her damp flesh. Her intense shudder filled him with anticipation for the weeks ahead, the adventure in store.

Summer opened the foil packet and handed the latex to him. "You do it."

"Don't you know—?"

"I know how to do it. Done it before,"

she said with a grin. "Banana."

A banana. Hell's teeth. And she called that experience? Bemused, he rolled the condom on and waited for her next move.

"Haven't done this next step before," she said cheerfully. "I figure you'll tell me if I don't do it right."

Her honesty was gonna kill him. Nikolai helped her guide his cock inside her pussy, eagerly waiting for her to impale herself. She did—inch by tortuous inch until he shook, so close to climax he was afraid to move. He took refuge in talk, trying to distract himself from the raw sensation stalking his body.

"Nothing we do together is wrong, or has a right or wrong way," he said through a surge of raw need.

Summer settled, fully impaled. She rocked in an experimental move. "I feel so full it almost hurts. But it's a good pain," she added. "What do I do now?"

Nikolai almost laughed. She asked for instructions now? Hell, if she did any better he'd internally combust. "Just move. Any way that feels good to you."

She lifted and sank downward. Her eyes drifted shut while her breasts bobbed in front of his face. "That feels good." She repeated the move and added a swivel of her hips. Her breath hissed out. "Sooo good."

Nikolai reached for a breast when it moved close to his face again. Her eyes flew open as he shaped the globe with his callused fingers then drew her pouting nipple into his mouth and sucked hard.

"Bite me," she said, rising until her nipple almost released from his mouth. The fire in his loins blazed. Higher.

Harder. Deeper. With each lazy rock of her hips, he bit down on her nipple, giving her enough teeth to transmit signals to her sex, but not hard enough to break any skin. Her entire body shook while her sweet pussy clasped him in sweet agony. He bit a little harder and pinched her other nipple. She tightened around his cock, and they gave a unified gasp of pleasure, his hips jerking, moving in counterpoint to her slow rocking. He released her breasts to grasp Summer's hips.

"Close?" he murmured.

"Mmmm." She arched her back, grinding her clit against the base of his cock.

Nikolai smoothed a finger across her clit, and she exploded, her pussy squeezing him rhythmically.

"Nikolai." Summer threw back her head

and growled her pleasure.

He thrust upward. Once. Twice. Hard and fast while her sheath clasped his dick in a silken grip. Climax burst through him, an explosion of heat that seemed to go on and on as he spurted his seed.

They fell on the bed together, Summer aligned along his body. Nikolai held her close, their bodies still joined. His eyes closed and he drifted into sleep.

Insistent thumping on Nikolai's front door pulled him awake. For an instant, he had no idea where he was, and then Summer's soft sigh clued him in. He moved her carefully off his chest and dealt with the condom that still cloaked his semi-limp cock.

"Not the smartest thing to go to

sleep like that," he said as thoughts of condom leakage filled his mind. Better not happen again.

Whoever was at his door leaned on the doorbell. He grabbed his jeans and yanked them up before hurrying down the passage leading to the front door.

Jake and Louie stood on the other side.

"I should have known," he groused, glaring at his mates. "What do you want?"

"Seems we caught Nik at a bad time." Jake wore a healthy smirk.

"Can we come in?"

"No," Nikolai said flatly.

Louie peered past Nikolai. "Do you have a guest?"

"Yes."

"A man of few words," Jake mused. "We want details."

"None of your bloody business. What

do you want?"

"Who do you have in your bed? I didn't think you let women into your house since Laura." Louie grinned so broadly Nikolai was tempted to hit him.

"Back off."

"I wonder if it's the babe," Jake said.

"Henry's niece?" Louie asked.

"Fuck off. Summer is here but not for the reasons you think," he said when their toothy grins widened. "Someone tried to run her off the road yesterday. Then they rang the hospital and told the receptionist they'd be in to visit. They told the nurse they were related. No one else knew she was there except the cops and Martin. Someone planted drugs in Henry's house and tattled to the cops. Summer is here for her protection, no other reason."

His friends sobered, but Louie's grin

took flight again without warning. "You know, Nik, I almost believe you." He leaned close and whispered, "But the babe looks as though she's had more than a sleep. In fact, if I was being crude, I'd say she'd had a good f—" The air exploded from his lungs, encouraged by Nikolai's fist applied to his stomach. He danced out of range to complete his sentence. "Fuck."

"No one asked you." Nikolai wanted to slam the door in his friends' faces, but the soft footsteps behind him indicated Summer had made an appearance. Nikolai smelled his soap as she stopped beside him. Desire kicked him in the gut when he glanced at her. Damp curls framed her face while her lips were red and swollen.

Damn, he'd wanted to share a shower. The first woman he'd ever met who took quick showers and he missed the occasion. His gaze wandered her body, noting she'd raided his wardrobe. The long navy-blue T-shirt plus the pair of black boxer shorts looked damn fine.

Taking advantage of his distraction, Louie pushed past him, and ran a quick hand across Summer's cheek. "Nik said someone tried to hurt you."

Nikolai suddenly felt very possessive. If Louie didn't step away, he risked an injury. He growled under his breath, but of course, Louie didn't back off.

Jake stepped inside his hallway too, taking Nikolai unawares and forcing him to take a step backward. His friend slung his arm around Summer's shoulders. "You okay, cupcake?"

"I'll make coffee," Nikolai muttered. No one took the slightest notice. With a last glare at Louie and Jake, he stomped into the kitchen.

Eventually, they all ended up sitting around his wooden table, nursing cups of black coffee—black being mandatory since the milk was off. Jake and Louie looked comfortable, as if they'd settled in for the duration. They chatted away with Summer and generally made themselves at home.

"Is there a reason for this visit?" Nikolai asked, doing his best to keep his voice calm. It didn't come off. He sounded plain testy.

"Captain wants us to go in this afternoon." Louie's gaze skimmed across Summer in silent warning.

"So, why are you here? I'm on sick leave."

"Captain wants you on the mission too."

Nikolai glanced across at Summer and

saw she was watching him. A faint smile twitched at her lips, and it made him wish his friends to Outer Siberia. The need to claim her lips leapt inside him, but the last thing he wanted was an audience, spectators who were likely to critique his performance.

Summer stroked her fingers across his forearm. Nikolai barely suppressed the shiver of awareness that raced through him. Damn, he had it bad. He was sick—definitely too ill to go on a mission. But no, that wasn't good either. Remember Henry.

The smile widened as if she read his confused thoughts. "You don't need to worry. I'll be fine."

"As far as I know, it's a strategy meeting," Louie said. "We'll be gone a few hours."

"No problem. What can happen in a few

hours?" Summer said.

Nikolai snorted. "Where you're concerned—quite a bit." She'd lived in Auckland for a few days short of a month and so far had hooked up with a gangster, had two break-ins, been taken in for questioning by the police and someone had run her off the road. And that was just for starters. Nikolai didn't intend to add losing her virginity to an older man to the list—not when he was trying to convince himself that sex didn't count in this situation since it was consensual.

"I'm not a child."

"No one implied you were." He glanced away from her to see Louie and Jake observing them closely. "How long? Two hours? Three? Okay. You've got my number. You can ring if you need us."

Summer watched the three men leave with something like relief. The testosterone in the kitchen had been so thick she'd thought about opening the window. It was the same when her brothers were at home with their friends. One on one was fine, but with a herd of the big he-men things could turn ugly, particularly if you were unlucky enough to be related to some of them.

She shut the front door and wandered into Nikolai's kitchen. The room was functional and basic with no feminine frills. The gray counter, the color of her father's goslings, which her mother muttered about tossing into the soup pot, and the teal-blue cupboard units were newly installed. Nikolai had furnished the floor with tiles a shade lighter than the counter. The wooden table in the middle of the tiled floor still needed sanding and varnishing. Add a few plants and a blind or some curtains and the place wouldn't look too bad.

From the little her uncle had told her about Nikolai, he'd purchased this house some time ago but hadn't started renovations until his recent sick leave. Nikolai's bedroom was completed, while the other rooms were stripped back to basics, waiting for a coat of paint and tender loving care.

She wrinkled her nose at the acrid paint scent. It was worse in this part of the house. Despite breathing in slow, shallow pants, the paint was affecting her breathing. Her chest tightened, her breathing strained enough for her to need her inhaler.

Summer collected her clothes from the

previous day along with her handbag and keys. After peering out the windows for a long time, checking for anything remotely suspicious, she decided it was safe. Living with SAS brothers and an uncle had taught her a thing or two—not to mention the Heroine's Handbook.

She let herself out of Nikolai's house, navigated the missing boards on his deck and ducked through the gate in the boundary fence.

The door was locked when she tried it, and nothing seemed out of place. She fished her keys from her bag, unlocked the door and stepped inside, flicking on the safety chain after she entered. First stop—her bedroom and an inhaler. The thought of an asthma attack hurried her along. She grabbed an inhaler off her dresser, took a quick puff and headed back to the kitchen.

A small red light flickered on the answering machine. Guilt stabbed her for an instant as she reached for the play button. She knew Nikolai wouldn't approve of her being here alone, but he wouldn't want her to have an asthma attack either. Nah, no problem. She had a cast-iron excuse if—when—he hollered.

Summer listened to the messages. Two heavy breathing calls. Charming. Then Dare's voice floated into the kitchen. "Summer, it's Dare here. I wondered how you were. I rang the hospital, but they said you'd gone home. I'm glad you're feeling better. I presume you're at work, so I'll ring you later this afternoon. Perhaps we could get together for dinner?"

Dare's message was the last one. She pressed the erase button and checked her watch. Maybe she should go to dinner with Dare and let him know she couldn't go out with him again. A frown wrinkled her brow at the thought. She'd slept with Nikolai and enjoyed it, but were they actually together?

Hard to say. She pulled a rueful face when confusion poured through her. But the truth stood out. If she wanted to go farther along Relationship Road with Nikolai, she needed to talk to Dare. She was a one-man-at-a-time kinda girl.

Decision made, she started to dial Dare's number before having second thoughts. It wasn't difficult to imagine Nikolai's reaction if she went out to dinner with Dare. Besides, she rather liked the idea of exploring more positions. There was an article in Miranda magazine, which offered lots of suggestions.

Summer picked up the phone again. She'd propose lunch and arrive back before Nikolai returned. What the big, bad SAS man didn't know wouldn't hurt him.

Or her.

Chapter 11

"Summer, how are you?" Dare rose from behind his desk and came around to greet her, hands outstretched in welcome. Dressed in a smart charcoal-gray suit with a black shirt and black-and-gray tie, he appeared handsome and successful.

But he wasn't Nikolai.

"I'm fine." She wondered how to avoid a kiss without making a big issue of it. Dare aimed for her lips and in the end, she turned her head, so his kiss landed on her cheek.

He grasped her hands in his and stood back to study her, seemingly unperturbed by her action. "I've tried ringing. Your phone was switched off. I wasn't sure if you were going to work or not."

"I slept in this morning." Summer felt the crawl of heat in her cheeks and knew she needed to change the subject fast. "Thanks for meeting me for lunch. I'm not a good invalid. Got bored with my own company." She found herself thinking about Nikolai's assertions—about Dare and his family's involvement in illegal activities. If criminal propensity was written on his face, she couldn't see it. He appeared the same as always.

Sophisticated. Attractive. Sexy.

Dare cleared his throat. "Do I need to wipe my face?"

She blinked, irritated at her transparency. Could she be any less subtle?

Amusement glittered in his eyes. "If there's lipstick on my face, it came from my mother. She popped in to see me about an hour ago."

Summer imagined her parents meeting Dare, and knew that although her mother was no pushover, she'd like him. Her father might take longer to warm to a man dating his daughter. Ditto her brothers.

"Sorry," Summer said, aware she was woolgathering yet again. "Are you ready to leave?"

"I'll let the restaurant staff know I'm going out then we're all set." He paused by the door to his office to smile at her. After tucking a curl behind her ear, he leisurely kissed her, taking her by surprise.

When they parted, she gasped for breath. Her pulse throbbed faster than

it had mere seconds ago. There had
to be something wrong with her. She'd
spent the morning in bed with Nikolai,
relished everything they'd done together
and wanted to repeat the experience,
yet kissing Dare was enjoyable too. A
topic for rapid thought because her
family wouldn't approve of her stringing
along two men. Heck, she disapproved
since the object of the luncheon exercise
was to end the budding relationship.

"You look beautiful," he murmured, his
eyes skimming her body.

She'd dressed carefully for the
meeting, needing to bolster her nerves.
Maybe she should have settled for
casual jeans and a shirt instead of her
favorite black skirt and the cream knit
top that clung to her breasts. Too late
now.

"Thanks." Summer nibbled her bottom

lip as she tried to think of the right way to put a halt to their romantic liaison yet remain friends. Not a single word came to mind.

Dare hustled her from his office with a warm hand at her waist. "I thought we'd have lunch at the Sky Tower today."

"Really?" Call her shallow, but she'd wanted to see the penis-shaped tower from the top. There hadn't been an opportunity so far. "That sounds great."

Minutes later, they were in a cab heading for the Sky Tower in Central Auckland.

"What are you doing for the rest of the day?" Dare asked.

"I'm not sure. I might stop by the bookstore on the way home. I want to see if my special order has arrived." She also intended to explore an adult shop and the different sex toys available, although she wasn't about to inform Dare of her plans.

An arc of energy buzzed from breast tips to her pussy at the idea of trying out toys and exploring her sexuality with the help of Nikolai. The naughty thought solved her dilemma.

Yes, while she enjoyed Dare's kisses, she hadn't once thought of him and sex toys in the same sentence. She'd let this thing with Nikolai run its course, whatever that might be, and take each day as it arrived. She found herself wriggling on the backseat while her heart jumped in acute anticipation.

Dare took possession of her hand, a small and private smile playing on his lips. "Were you a hyperactive child?"

"Not as bad as my brothers."

"Hmm. I think I'd like to meet them."

Summer didn't think so. "I enjoyed

meeting your family," she said, changing the subject.

"I was sorry about being called away on business." Dare picked up her hand and pressed a kiss on her wrist. It tickled, making her uncomfortably aware of her body and the way her knit top clung to her breasts.

The cab pulled up outside Sky Tower. Thank goodness. He'd have to let her go. The man hadn't acted so touchy-feely on previous dates. Yes, he'd kissed her but he hadn't acted with such possessiveness. What was going on here? Whatever it was, his actions were doing her head and giving her pulse a hell of a roller coaster ride.

He climbed from the cab, helped her out and paid the driver. Taking her arm, he held her close to his side, and whisked her into the Sky Hotel. Then they were in the lift speeding to the top of the tower.

"Wow, that was quick." Summer yanked her hand from Dare's warm grasp to clutch her stomach. "I think I left my tummy on the ground floor," she said with a rueful smile.

They stepped from the lift and walked straight into the restaurant.

"Is this the revolving restaurant?" She peered out the closest window in awe. Auckland harbor stretched out in front of her with the dormant island volcano of Rangitoto in the foreground. Boats of all shapes and sizes dotted the blue water. It was no wonder people called it the city of sails. To her left was a marina of yachts while to her right a cruise ship disgorged tourists for their Auckland stopover. She turned to Dare. "Thank you for bringing me. The view is breathtaking."

A pleased smile softened his mouth. "I thought you'd enjoy it here. Once we get to our table, I'll point out some of the sights for you."

They were seated and had drinks before she had time to blink. She picked up her tall glass of orange juice and took a quick sip to wash away the dry cotton nerves in her mouth.

Dare consulted the menu and ordered for them without bothering to check her preferences.

"How do you know what I wanted to eat?" She didn't bother to hide the tartness in her voice. He'd done this before.

"I don't have much time. It speeds things up if I order."

The man was a control freak in all facets of his life as she was learning.

Each date underlined the annoying habit a bit more.

"Would you like to go out to dinner tonight?" he asked, ignoring her protest in typical fashion.

"I'm sorry. Not tonight."

"I'll drop in and see you on the way home."

Summer gaped at his handsome countenance. Bottle Top Bay was a little out of his way.

"Not tonight," she said.

"I won't stay long. Just long enough to reassure myself you're okay."

His words made her nervous. Was he going to turn out to be one of those weird stalkers? A man who refused to take a hint? Her stomach flipped with an attack of anxiety. It was easy to imagine her family's reaction. And Nikolai's.

"I think we should slow things down

between us. I'm not ready for anything serious. I'm too young." She cringed inwardly and was glad Nikolai and her family weren't present to hear her excuses.

"Can you see the marina down there?" Dare asked.

Summer gaped. Was that it? That had been English coming from her mouth, not a foreign language. "Yes."

"We keep our boat there. You'll have to come out with us one weekend."

"Us?" Crooks used boats to run drugs, didn't they?

"My brothers and me. We use the boat mainly, but sometimes my sisters or parents come out."

"Where do you go?"

"We visit the islands around the Hauraki Gulf or sometimes farther afield."

Summer's mind was stuck on drugs, and crime and Nikolai. But mostly Nikolai, because she knew how furious he'd become when he discovered the name of her lunch companion.

"What do you say?"

"I... Maybe."

The meals arrived—a large steak and a selection of vegetables. Summer would have preferred the portabella mushrooms and rice but picked at the vegetables.

Dare kept up a steady stream of conversation, talking about the movies they should see and the restaurants he wanted to check out with her in attendance.

"I need some time to study. And I have to work several late nights now that I've settled in my job."

"We'll work around your

commitments," Dare said.

His words stumped her because Miranda magazine hadn't covered this situation. She'd tried the nice approach, the polite approach. Tried blunt too. What part of not interested didn't the man understand? She placed her knife and fork across the center of her plate and dropped her napkin on top.

"Good. You're finished." Dare stood and strode over to the desk to pay for the meal, leaving her in stunned astonishment.

In the lift, he took her arm and stood close. One of the ingredients in his sophisticated aftershave didn't agree with her, tickling at the back of her nose. A sneeze burst free. Dare stepped back, giving her room to breathe.

"Excuse me," she said. "There's something in your aftershave that doesn't agree with me." Okay, that was blunt.

Dare steered her from the lift, up the ramp and outside. A cab appeared magically, and they climbed inside.

"Parnell Road, please," he told the driver.

When they arrived at Dare's restaurant, he gave her money.

"That's to pay for your cab fare home. You still going to the bookshop first?"

Summer nodded dumbly.

Dare leaned inside and kissed her on the mouth, rattled the address off to the driver and stood back. At the last moment, he knocked on the window, and she pushed the button to make it open.

"Sorry I haven't been good company today. My mind is on business, I'm afraid." He slipped two more fifties out of his wallet and handed them to her. "My order is in. Can you pick it up for me? I'll collect it when we go out to dinner tonight." He bent to give her another quick kiss and strode away.

She stared after his rapidly retreating form. What was all that about?

"Are you ready to go now?" the cabby asked.

"Yes, thank you." She settled back to puzzle out Dare's behavior. No matter what way she looked at their outing, she came up with the same thought.

Weird. Extremely weird.

Ten minutes later, she entered the bookshop. Miranda magazine was in as were several of the romances from her order plus Dare's package. She paid for them all, caught another cab and headed for home.

"Where the hell have you been?"

The masculine holler scared three myna birds from their food quest in Uncle Henry's garden. They took off with indignant squawks while she attempted to control the spurt of panic that made her stomach do backflips.

Nikolai stood on his section, glaring across the wooden fence. She aimed for calm as she stooped to pull a pair of wet jeans from the laundry basket.

"Doing the laundry." Although she would have thought her purpose clear, given she was hanging it on the line to dry.

Nikolai stomped out of sight before reappearing on Uncle Henry's side of the fence. "You were meant to stay inside my house for safety reasons. Remember?"

"The paint smell was affecting my breathing."

"You didn't have a problem last night. Or this morning."

If Summer had thought she was attracted to Dare and was in danger of becoming a two-man woman, then one look at Nikolai cured her of the misapprehension. Nikolai, bossy gene and all, was her man of the month—for as long as he wanted her.

The man scowled. A flash of heat speared through her body. The air charged between them. Sexual sparks, full of possibilities.

"No problem at all." Oh, my. Her voice—it sounded like a sultry screen siren, throaty and flirty. Turned-on.

Nikolai stepped nearer until warmth jumped from his body to hers. Her nipples tightened against the cotton cups of her bra. Then he closed the remaining distance between them, and her nipples crushed against his chest. Her breath whooshed from her lungs, and nothing replaced the air. She felt breathless, and it had nothing to do with her asthma.

He glanced down at her, his blunt finger traced over her bottom lip. His dark eyes glittered. "So, where have you been?"

Summer opened her mouth to speak, and his finger popped right between her lips. Acting on instinct, she sucked lightly and rolled her tongue across the tip. A low groan erupted from him, and his eyes fluttered shut, a pained expression creasing his brow. Then his eyes snapped open again. Heat, dark and stormy, surged between them.

"Hey, man! I thought you said five

minutes."

"Go away," Nikolai growled without turning.

Summer released his finger but couldn't take her gaze off him. What she wanted more than anything was to rip off his clothes and touch him. Of course, he'd need to do some fondling in return.

"Hell, Louie and I wouldn't want to miss the show," Jake said.

Louie chuckled with real amusement, and she saw the waggle of his dark brows, the humor glinting in his expression. "Yeah, not when you're about to rip off each other's clothes. Things are getting interesting."

Nikolai's broad chest rose and fell with a harsh breath. "Later," he whispered. "I have to go out for a few hours." His hands tangled in her hair, and he lowered his head as if he were about to kiss her. "Please lock the door when we leave. With you inside," he added.

"Okay. I'll be at Uncle Henry's house. The paint is bothering me."

Nikolai nodded, and despite the audience, he lowered his head until their mouths touched. Bold lips stole her breath, and his tongue surged into her mouth. She wrapped her arms around his neck and held on tight. Finally, he lifted his head.

"Stay safe," he murmured.

She nodded solemnly and stood on tiptoe to whisper in his ear. "I visited an adult shop today."

His hands closed over her shoulders. "A sex shop?"

Louie whistled long and low. "Did you hear that, Jake? A sex shop. Sounds like our Nik is in for some fun."

"Out the front," Nikolai snapped. "Wait

for me there."

The two men went but not without big grins and banter.

Nikolai waited until they'd walked past the rose garden and disappeared around the corner of the house. He took her face between his hands. "What am I going to do with you?" A slow smile spread from his eyes down to his mouth. "Should I be worried?"

"About the toys I bought?"

His forehead wrinkled in a quick frown. "Yeah."

Silent laughter bubbled up inside her as she thought of the vibrator, the selection of condoms, including glow-in-the-dark green, and the set of pleasure balls. "Nothing too radical."

"That is what I'm afraid of. I'm thinking your radical and mine are miles apart."

An impatient honk sounded as one of

his friends leaned on the horn.

Nikolai leaned close, flicking his fingers over her distended nipples hard enough that she jumped. "Don't start playtime without me."

Even though Summer was aware of the jut of his cock, his smoky voice would have given him away. She flashed a grin. "Don't be late, big boy."

"Big boy." His words came close to an undignified splutter. "One of these days, I'm gonna smack your luscious backside."

"So you keep saying," she chortled, enjoying the novelty of sexual banter. "I look forward to it."

"Humph!" Nikolai said, but he kissed her before he strode off to join his friends.

The rest of the afternoon passed quickly enough. Summer caught up on chores and watered Uncle Henry's rose gardens.

The phone rang around six thirty.

"Summer, I'm sorry. Something's come up, and I can't make our dinner date," Dare said.

"But I—" She inhaled sharply. Was he deaf? Her breath huffed out again. "Thanks for letting me know."

"I've got to go. I'll ring you."

The phone thudded down. A frisson of unease skittered down her backbone. Dare Martin was a successful businessman. The man wasn't stupid, so why was he acting obtuse? She hated to admit it, but it seemed Nikolai might be right in his warnings.

She replaced the phone and wandered over to check out the contents of the fridge. Nothing looked inspiring. She slammed the door shut and reached for the kettle.

Two minutes later, Summer sat outside on the deck with a cup of peppermint tea at her side and her parcel of new books.

Summer reached into the paper carry bag and pulled out a thick book first. Fly-Fishing in New Zealand. It was identical to the first book she'd received in error earlier in the month. Brow puckered, she opened the pages at random, flicking past illustrations of fish and feathery hooks. Why would Dare buy two copies of the same book? And even stranger, Dare preferred the cut and thrust of the business world. He never walked when he could ride. The thought of him in the great outdoors up to his waist in cold water boggled her mind.

Chapter 12

Nikolai hadn't arrived home by midnight. Disappointed, but trying hard to contain her unhappiness, she put down her book and switched off the bedside lamp.

The house creaked and groaned with comforting familiarity, and she drifted closer to sleep. The abrupt rattle of the wooden window frame jerked her rigid. Her skin crawled. Her eyes flipped open while every muscle locked. The frame squeaked as the intruder raised it fully.

Summer slid her legs from under the quilt and prepared to leap for the door. A black shadow blotted out the light as it maneuvered through the window. On trembling legs, she stood.

The doors were locked, just as Nikolai had ordered. She was positive she'd locked the window as well. Too late to double-check.

A sharp creak broke the agonizing silence. Terror clamped around her chest. Everything moved in slow motion. The figure stepped toward the bed.

Summer stared in fascinated horror and edged toward the door. He was undoing his trousers. "I-is that you, Nikolai?"

"Who else would it be?" a recognizable masculine voice demanded. "I'd better not find anyone else coming in that window."

Her shoulders sagged before she straightened to flick on the bedside lamp. She planted her hands on her hips. "You scared the shit out of me. Why didn't you ring the doorbell? Like a normal person."

"Checking the security."

In the dim light cast by the lamp, she caught the dopey smirk on his face. Suspicion narrowed her eyes. "You've been drinking."

The louse. And to think she'd worried about him.

She kept her gaze off his bare torso—the well-muscled chest and the set of wide shoulders that tapered down to a narrow waist with not a trace of excess padding. She would not weaken despite the temptation, not with a point to prove. She was no commodity to be taken for granted.

The grin widened to broad. "Not too much that I can't get it up."

He wouldn't be getting anything up anywhere. She sniffed, turned her back in a pointed manner, crawled back into bed and tugged the covers up to her chin. "Turn off the light on your way out."

"Oh, no. No, sweetheart." Nikolai's hands went back to the zipper on his jeans. It rasped downward, and she averted her gaze. Clothing rustled before silence reigned.

Summer strained to hear. Bother. She shouldn't have closed her eyes. All her senses were registering off the Richter scale. Her imagination. Just thinking about running her hands over his golden flanks, across his broad chest, spiked her temperature. Thinking about his cock and the way it had felt thrusting inside her.

All of a sudden, the mattress depressed. Her eyes popped open and came face-to-groin. His cock was fully erect, the head a deep plum red. As he'd said, primed and ready for action.

"You couldn't ring?" she squeaked. It was difficult to remain calm and dignified with a one-eyed snake staring her straight in the face.

Nikolai slid under the covers, stretched out and pulled their bodies flush. "The meeting went late."

"You can't take me for granted, can't expect me to wait for you."

"You didn't wait for me today." His brown eyes bore into her as if searching for truth. She held the connection, even though she felt like a mouse baited by a cocksure cat. But lucky for her, she'd learned a thing or two from watching Tom and Jerry cartoons.

"I'm not a quick f…flip for you to use whenever the timing fits your schedule."

His dark brows danced up and down, but he didn't crack a smile. "Flip?"

Habit made Summer sneak a look over

her shoulder. "My mother trained us well. Four letter words starting with f and ending with k are banned in our house. She has an endless supply of soap bars and a strong arm. Ask my brothers if you don't believe me."

A slow, sexy smile crawled across his mouth, and her heart pumped out an extra beat. Oh my. The man needed a license for that grin.

"I'll make sure I guard my mouth when I meet your parents." His hand cruised across her ribs to settle on her hipbone.

Okay. Now he'd confused her. In truth, she hadn't thought much past her six-month visit to Auckland. Her family assumed she'd go home to Eketahuna at the end of the library course.

Nikolai fondled her bottom. "You going to show me your toys? Or do you want to save them for when we have more time?"

"More time?"

"Jake and Louie are picking me up at six tomorrow morning. We have to go out of town for a couple of days."

Disappointment surged through her, and she must have made a sound because he pressed his lips to her forehead.

"I'm not happy about it myself. I don't want to leave you on your own. Not with the weird things that have been happening."

"I'll be fine. I followed your stringent security instructions to the letter." Apart from going out to see Dare.

"Jake said you could go and stay with his sister."

"No, I promised Uncle Henry I'd look after his house and his precious roses. I'll be all right here."

"You are so much like Henry, it's scary."

"You wouldn't be in bed, naked, with Henry." The shudder that swept him brewed a giggle. It bubbled from her, easing the subdued mood that had fallen between them at the talk of her safety.

"Hell, no! Henry was my boss. A mate. The picture... Hell, that's downright unsettling."

A Tom and Jerry moment. How to distract a male in one easy lesson. She wanted to blow on her finger and ceremoniously mark an imaginary scorecard. She resisted.

"How are you feeling? The lump on your head isn't as swollen."

"That was sneaky."

"I'm not in the military for nothing."

"Don't remind me," Summer said.

"You tired?"

"Not really."

"Good." He rolled without warning, taking her with him. Summer ended up lying on top of his hard body, his erection trapped between them.

"New position?" she asked, the sultry film-star voice making a return appearance.

"We have time to experiment."

"How about sex outside? That sounds like fun." She licked her lips and watched him closely.

"Baggage." Nikolai slapped her on the rump.

Summer froze. The slap and resulting sting on her butt should have fueled anger. Instead, her pussy tingled pleasantly. Juices moistened the juncture of her thighs. The need to kiss him, to taste him became more important than banter or scoring points.

She lowered her head and covered his quirking lips with hers. A hint of whiskey, smoky and suggestive of peat, tickled her taste buds. She took the kiss deeper, swirling their tongues together and exploring the softness of his inner cheek. A quick punch of heat tightened her nipples, until she ached.

While their mouths mated, Nikolai's hand slid in a long, luxurious stroke down her back, ending on her butt cheeks. He palmed them and slid a finger down the crack between, skimming across sensitive nerve endings.

She moaned in pleasure.

"You like that? Me touching your arse and fingering your pussy."

Words failed her so she nodded, her heart beating with acute anticipation. Nikolai moved again, exhibiting raw strength as he lifted and rolled her smoothly beneath him.

He grinned down at her. "Then you'll like this too. Warm up before we get to the good stuff."

Whatever. It all sounded good, and the talented fingers running over her limbs felt even better.

He slid one leg between hers and bent to press wet kisses across her aching breasts. She explored him too, running her hands over bulging muscles and his strong back, but she waited for him to close his mouth over her breasts. She craved the sweet ache as his lips circled her nipple. The fierce tug. The faint bite of teeth.

Her nails dug into his back as he continued to tease, kissing around the edge of her nipple, coming close but not close enough.

"Nikolai?"

"Yeah?"

"Open your mouth."

He grinned up at her, tousled and sexy as hell. "Like this?" he teased, opening his mouth and shutting it seconds later.

"No, not like that." Frustrated, she decided to tell him what she wanted and how she wanted it. "Open your mouth like this. Leave it open."

Humor glinted in his dark eyes. "Dangerous if there are mosquitoes around." But he followed her instructions.

Summer shoved her nipple in his mouth.

"You can shut your mouth now," she said.

Nikolai laughed, and her nipple popped from his mouth. Damp from saliva, it glistened. The humor left him, and he took her between his lips again. Soft suction speared a bolt of lust all the way to her toes.

She bit her lip, in a bit of a daze. They hadn't gotten anywhere near the good stuff and already she shivered on the cusp of climax. She wondered if that made her easy, then shoved the thought away.

Nikolai moved his leg, widening her stance. Cool air contrasted with the warmth of her pussy as he swept the covers aside. He mouthed her nipple a little more roughly, and a hungry noise escaped her. She stirred restlessly, needing more, needing the emptiness filled by him.

Only Nikolai.

But he seemed determined to tease her to breaking point, to make her plead.

He released her nipple and kissed

across her quivering belly. The stubble on his jaw contrasted with the lash of his tongue and shoved her into a heavy fog of desire. Her breath caught...until her lungs burned.

"Better breathe, sweetheart. Don't want to explain a faint to the medical staff."

She gasped, with both indignation and the desperate need for air.

He parted her folds, his gaze traveling unhurriedly across her feminine flesh. "So pretty." Satisfaction and hunger slashed his sensual mouth, a hint of his captivating smile.

She knew it.

He intended to tease her more, push her further. She opened her mouth to complain, but a trace of sensation drifted along her cleft, a warm puff of air. Her hips jerked while her heart slammed her ribs.

"So quick to respond." He glanced up at her, devilment on his face. "Are you sure you haven't spent the evening playing with these new toys I've been hearing about?"

Her head thrashed from side to side, the pillow throwing out the scent of lavender. It was meant to calm, but she was too far gone for the benefits of aromatherapy. "No, I wanted to wait for you."

"Maybe we should play."

A snort escaped. "That's what I've been trying to tell you."

"Ah, but you didn't say the words. I'm not a mind reader." Laughter shaded his voice. She wanted to deck him. She wanted to scream. Most of all she wanted to climax.

"Just as I'd always suspected," she said,

propping herself up on her elbows to glare at him. "You soldier types only do orders. Fine. This is your objective. An orgasm for me." She patted her breastbone. "Do your worst."

He chuckled long and loud, each successive gasp and breath of air puffing out of his lungs and hitting her achy clit. Finally, his laughter subsided, and he gave a lopsided salute. "Aye-aye, ma'am. My pleasure, ma'am."

"Well, hurry, soldier." Outwardly, she sounded bossy, calm and in control. Inside, she was anything but. Her skin temperature felt off the scale and hot enough to melt a knob of butter.

She imagined butter running over her belly, dripping down... Nikolai licking. Maybe chocolate sounded better, with her tongue doing the chasing over smooth, bulging muscles. A whimper escaped before she could catch it.

Nikolai spread her legs wider, then paused to study her quizzically. "Fantasizing, sweetheart?"

"Because you're not going fast enough."

"Tell me about this fantasy or I'll take things even slower." His finger dipped past her entrance and rotated with delicate precision. He lifted it to his mouth and made a soft smacking sound as he licked away her juices. "You're wet. I know you're ready to take me, but some self-control and restraint on your part will make your orgasm better."

"You're a sadist."

He slid his hands between her butt and the cotton sheet and lifted her to his mouth. "I intend to sip and savor," he whispered in a husky voice. "Enjoy the entrée before the main course."

Each warm breath blasted against her inflamed flesh. She trembled, her heart beating so loudly it was difficult to take in his bold, sensual words.

"God, Nikolai!" His rough words wrapped her in sensation. Tingling from head to toe, she shuddered. Her eyes slid closed, enclosing her in a private world of bliss.

Pure feeling. Acute expectation.

"Open your eyes. I want to see the expression in your beautiful eyes when you come." A finger stroked down her cleft but didn't venture near her clitoris.

Summer tried to follow his instructions—orders—but her lids felt weighted, too heavy to lift.

The stroking ceased. "Summer."

Yep, definitely orders. Her eyes struggled to half-mast.

Nikolai replaced his finger with the tip

of his tongue. A delicate flutter. A slow thrust and retreat.

She gave up the fight and let her eyes drift shut. Instantly the sensation of his tongue flickering against her flesh halted. A deep-seated throb pierced her languor. Her eyes shot open.

He hummed in approval and licked the length of her weeping cleft, stopping just short of her clit. The throb repeated, radiating outward from her nub. At the next stroke, she jerked her hips, and his tongue lashed her clitoris. A soft, prickling heat rushed through her, but this time she remembered and fought to keep her eyes open, her gaze locked on Nikolai's intent face.

Sexual hunger stabbed her mind, her body. All over. "Again, Nikolai. Please."

He chuckled as his finger stroked again, but this time instead of stopping, his digit continued its journey and feathered over her needy clit. A jagged sensation streaked the length of her body. She arched into his touch, aching for more, for total, body-pulsing ecstasy.

"Greedy little thing."

"Not little."

"Notice you're not denying the greedy," he drawled, doing another pass with his finger.

"Damn straight," she gritted out.

The third pass of his finger made tingles spring to life. They spread outward from her clit in a soft wave. She bit her bottom lip, preparing to fly, but the sensations dissolved. Disappointment bopped her over the head. Was that it?

She relaxed in Nikolai's hold, her gaze remaining locked to his.

"At last," he said in a guttural voice.

"Surrender."

Before she could react, he lifted her higher and sealed his mouth around her clit. A gentle flick of his tongue against her swollen core brought the fizzing anticipation back with a roar. Her hips jerked as he flailed her clitoris. Once. Twice. Three times. She exploded with a wallop of heat, shards of sensation rocketing to every pleasure point.

Gradually, she came to her body again. She'd kept her gaze on Nikolai the entire time, but only now did she register the fiery heat in him, the promise.

"Tell me you have condoms," he said in a hoarse voice.

Summer batted her eyelashes. "I could say no, but I wouldn't do that to you."

"Only because you want me to fuck you."

Summer nodded thoughtfully, and

manfully hid her smirk. "Yes, there is that. Top drawer, in the cellophane bag."

Nikolai lowered her hips to the mattress and bounded off the bed. He yanked the wooden drawer open, rifled through the bag and pulled out an unopened box. He turned to her with a frown, totally unconscious of his body in a way she admired. From this angle, his cock appeared huge. Pre-cum glistened on the tip, and just like that, she was hot, achy and desperate for his touch.

"Hurry," she urged as she took in the scars around his knee.

His brows shot toward his hairline. "Glow-in-the-dark, Summer?"

"Yeah."

"Neon green?"

"It was a toss-up between glow-in-the-dark, chocolate flavored or raised dots for great stimulation."

"What happened to normal, everyday condoms?"

"They left along with your sense of adventure?"

Nikolai ripped open the packet and pulled out a foil-covered square. For a few seconds, he stared at the bright green package. "You tell anyone about this, I'll deny it."

"I wouldn't dare," she deadpanned.

Nikolai bared a set of white teeth in a low growl, but she witnessed the humor lurking beneath. "On your stomach," he ordered. "Up on all fours."

"Oh! A new position."

"Yeah, the spanking position. Because I sure as hell haven't met any woman who needs a spanking more than you."

"I've heard across the man's knees is better."

He groaned. "If you don't shut up, I'm

gonna gag you as well."

"Tie me up? Oh, I like the sound of that!"

The foil wrapper crackled. A snort escaped, and she noticed another imperceptible shake of his head. "They're the color of an ogre."

"Is that what you call it?" She stared fixedly at his cock, taking delight in the twitch she witnessed. "Ogre."

"Your mother didn't wash your mouth out nearly enough."

"Enough that I don't enjoy the taste of soap."

He rolled on the condom and prowled to the edge of the bed.

Summer flicked off the bedside lamp. She stared at his erection, a long, thick batten that glowed neon green. "They work!"

The disapproving snort of a man pushed almost to the limits bounced off her bedroom walls. She positioned herself on her knees, still smirking. Nikolai cupped the round globes of her buttocks, his thumbs skirting close to her entrance. The laughter left her, a groan trembling free instead.

"This is gonna be hard and quick."

Summer felt cool air on her labia, her clit, as he parted her folds. His cock nudged her opening, then he surged deep with a seamless stroke. Shock at the sudden filling stole her breath. Wide and thick, he stretched her almost painfully. A good pain. His balls slapped her backside as he pulled out to thrust deep again.

Fast. Hard. Satisfying.

The scent of their arousal filled the air. A rough growl vibrated in his chest. Flesh smacked against flesh. The familiar tingle commenced as he plunged inside her, scraping across her sensitive core.

Summer teetered on the edge of climax, her heart thundering. Nikolai's hands curled around the dip of her waist and moved higher to palm heavy breasts. He pinched a nipple, his fingers biting enough to draw her gasp. He tugged and her channel contracted.

"That's it, sweetheart." He squeezed her distended nipple, and she exploded into a series of intense spasms. He slammed into her once more and stilled, his breathing hoarse, his chest rising and falling against her sweaty back.

Summer twitched her butt, rocking back against him. Sated and sleepy, the pleasure continued to hum through her veins like syrup. So good.

Nikolai drew a deep breath. When he'd entered via the window, he hadn't bothered drawing the curtains and a stream of moonlight pierced the shadowed corners of the room. His gaze traced the sweet dip of her waist, the rounded arse cheeks, and guilt surfaced. He'd made a mistake fucking her. She was too young, and everything, every relationship he'd had in the past had turned to murky custard. The fact remained—he sucked at relationships, but even knowing that, he wasn't sure he could walk away. Not now.

She'd forgotten to tell Nikolai about the fishing book. She skipped a couple of steps and came to a stop by the kettle. Her hands grabbed the marbled countertop. A breath whooshed from her. With a grimace, she did a quick series of breathing exercises. Gradually, she straightened and gave an embarrassed laugh. Thank goodness, that breathing hitch had happened while she'd been alone.

Summer went through the automatic motions of making tea and mused over the situation. Nikolai's fault for distracting her this morning. It wasn't as though she fired on all cylinders in the mornings anyway. But today she'd been semi-awake when Nikolai yanked the covers off the bed. She grinned as she recalled his wolfish expression, how rough and rumpled he'd looked.

Her heart pounded anew from the memory. Chocolate-coated sex on a stick. The man had picked her up and carried her to the shower where he'd proceeded to wash her with the Brazil nut shower gel she kept in the shower. Once he'd finished, he'd briskly washed himself and pulled on a glow-in-the-dark condom.

She squirmed, shifting from one foot to the other. The kettle whistled and switched off. Her hand shook as she reached for it. Deep breaths. She inhaled, seeking control of her wayward emotions.

Sex. And Nikolai.

She seemed to dwell on them a lot these days. A shiver worked down her body, ending in an intense ache in her core. Arousal soaked her panties despite making love before Nikolai left. She had to get a grip. But Nikolai hadn't helped. He'd dared her, and she never backed away from a challenge.

In the shower, he'd turned her around so her back was to him. He'd pressed her palms on the white tiled wall and crowded her from behind. The water had spilled over them, warm and steamy, and scented with Brazil nut. Then, he'd entered her from behind, and Summer had thought she might expire on the spot.

Her pulse jumped and she stayed herself from picking up the kettle. Not yet when she trembled so much. Her clit tingled as she recalled, as she relived the quick thrusts and the blast of pleasure. Nikolai filling her, surrounding her with his strength, propelling her into a climax that shuddered through her body for long seconds afterward.

Then he'd withdrawn, slapped her on the arse and turned her around for a possessive kiss.

But it hadn't ended there. He'd washed her again and shut off the shower. In the steamy intimacy of the bathroom, he'd dried her and disappeared. Seconds later, he'd returned with one of the toys she'd purchased in the adult shop on K Road. The set of pleasure balls. With an intent look in his eyes, he'd pulled them from the packet and slowly inserted them into her pussy.

Summer shifted from foot to foot. Her core contracted suddenly. He'd instructed her to think of him during the day. How could she not?

Every step she took made the weighted balls vibrate. The sheer naughtiness factor turned her on just as much as the pulsing movement of the balls.

She picked up the kettle again and successfully poured a cup of tea. She perched on the edge of a wooden chair and took a sip.

Back to the book. It was in her straw basket, ready to drop off for Dare at the restaurant. A frown puckered her smooth brow as she stared at the paper bag containing the duplicate book. What if Nikolai was right? What if Dare was using her for some ulterior motive?

Summer considered the indigestible fact for a few moments longer. Then an idea occurred, simplicity itself.

She could exchange the book for another of the same—that was assuming she could find one. After twisting the idea in every possible direction, it sounded even better. The reckless rebel inside her rejoiced at the thought of doing something constructive. This was a simple plan to prove or disprove Nikolai's theory about the Martin family.

About Dare.

The perfect plan.

And it would work.

She wrapped her hands around her cup and congratulated herself on her cleverness. She was sure that in a week or two she could rub Nikolai's nose in the fact.

The soldier would have to bend and get with her program.

Chapter 13

Later that day

The hairs at her nape prickled. Summer's entire body pulsed with uneasiness until she wanted to jump like a rabbit. The desire to spin around and demand whoever was following her to piss off hammered through her brain, finding an outlet in clenched fists.

But she didn't have soldier brothers for nothing. She knew a thing or two about subtlety. A snort escaped. Well, they were restrained and canny when it came to their work. Ditto Nikolai.

Just thinking about Nikolai made her hips sway a fraction more than normal and the pleasure balls seemed to vibrate with more vigor inside her pussy.

She paused to survey the contents of a large department store. Instead of looking at the clothes, she scanned reflections in the window. Nothing out of the ordinary. But that didn't mean no one was there. She trusted her instincts. Perhaps she should tell Nikolai. Except he was sure to start yelling and ram a few "I told you so"s into the conversation. Of course, when he started shouting she could always try distraction.

After scanning the colorful swimsuits in the window, and the reflections of the passersby, she continued, heading for one of the three secondhand bookshops she sometimes frequented.

The bookshop was small, the shelves crammed to overflowing with books of all shapes and sizes. The bell on the door tinkled when she pushed it open. She took a deep breath, the book lover in her enjoying the dry, musty scent that permeated the room. Heaven.

Hustling, she wove between the shelves, scanning for the section on hobbies and fishing. Not a single book on fly-fishing. She nibbled her bottom lip, considering her options. It wouldn't do to order one since she was time-challenged. The thin, elderly man behind the counter wasn't a good option either, since she didn't want anyone remembering her asking for the book. Time to try the next shop on her list.

Twenty minutes later, she rushed inside. Luckily, she was a frequent visitor and was familiar with the layout of the cavern-like shop. Summer checked her watch. Heck, she was going to be late back from lunch. Mrs. Ferguson would have two cows. She did that. A lot.

The shelf space allocated to fishing took up a whole section of shelving in the narrow shop. She scrutinized the titles but almost missed the fly-fishing book in her haste.

Her stomach lurched when she spotted the title. It was there. She pulled the book off the shelf, her heart thudding erratically.

The point of no return.

If she bought the book, she was committing to the plan.

"Earth to Nik. Earth to Nik." Louie clicked his fingers right in front of Nikolai's nose.

Nikolai blinked back to the present, away from black thoughts of Laura and the baby. Nightmares tangled with the future and Summer. "Huh?"

Jake peered closely. "He looks tired."

"Perhaps he didn't sleep well." Louie smirked at Jake. "Wonder how Summer slept?"

"Leave her out of this," Nikolai growled.

"You didn't stay out of Summer."

A wave of fury swept him, and he had his hands fisted in Jake's shirt before either of his mates could blink.

"Whoa." Jake held up both hands in surrender but didn't try to struggle from Nikolai's determined grip. "Joke."

Louie placed a heavy hand on Nikolai's tense shoulder. "Let him go, Nik."

He unclenched his hands and shoved Jake away. A fist-size circle of wrinkles remained on Jake's shirt.

"Sorry, man. Bad joke."

Nikolai didn't want to discuss Summer with Jake and Louie. "Time to get back to the rest of the men." Hell, he was kicking himself as it was. He didn't need his mates' help to fuel his betrayal and helplessness. Nikolai turned and stomped back to the assault course, leaving Jake and Louie to fall in behind while he tried to ignore the throb of his knee.

What the fuck was he going to do? He'd betrayed Henry's trust, taken Summer's virginity, and he continued to compound the bitch of a mistake. He couldn't keep his hands off her.

But the worst part was the way his mind wandered to the future—a rosy dream of togetherness. Nikolai bit back a curse. He'd once dreamed of a future, a family with Laura, and look what had happened. While he'd been away on missions, Laura had got bored, felt neglected. So she'd gone out on the town, made friends with a bad crowd—people who treated drugs like candy. Bittersweet memories poured over him as he recalled the moment he and Laura had discovered her pregnancy. Their child would have been almost five, ready to start school.

A lump of emotion clogged his throat. He blinked and called upon every shred of his control. He had a mission to complete. Now wasn't the time to dwell on what might have been.

She'd done it. Exchanged books. Nerves pushed a shiver through her limbs as the cab drove up Parnell Road. Summer stared out the window at the rush hour traffic, the scurrying office workers heading home and the mature trees in the Domain. Please, please let her pull off the switch without making Dare suspicious. The cab pulled up outside the restaurant. She paid the driver and dawdled inside. Even the pleasure balls vibrating inside her pussy didn't quell the skip and jump of anxiety.

A wave of chatter greeted her as she pushed through the double doors leading to the bar and restaurant.

A man standing in a group at the bar gave a long whistle. "Over here, sweet cheeks." His gaze raked up and down, taking in her short black skirt and V-neck navy-blue top.

Summer ignored him, too wound up to flirt. Her heels clicked as she maneuvered through the crowd waiting to enter. She approached the reception desk once the large group of people waiting disappeared into a private function room.

"Is Dare busy?"

"Afraid so, Summer," the receptionist

said.

Summer nodded and tried to look disappointed, but in fact, everything was going according to plan. "Can I leave a package for him? I promised him I'd drop it off." She handed over the book and was glad when another group of diners arrived behind her. "Looks like you're busy so I'll leave you to it." She lifted a hand in farewell.

"Bye, Summer. I'll make sure Dare gets his package."

Outside on the pavement, she took a deep breath and reached for the nearest streetlamp to steady the sway of wobbly knees.

Had she done the right thing?

She sighed, unsure of her actions. But at least if Dare made a fuss, it would confirm her suspicions. She scanned the road for a cab. The prickly sensation that came from watchful eyes recommenced. The sooner she arrived home, the better. Along with the edginess caused by surveillance and burning anxiety, the pleasure balls had her so hot it was a wonder she hadn't burned from the inside out.

Nikolai pulled up in front of his house after returning from their out-of-town training session. His knee ached like the devil, letting him know he'd pushed too hard. He needed a shower. Bad. He stunk like the bottom of a sewer pit after running the obstacle course through mud and God knows what else. But at least they were prepared for the mission. It was good to be involved again, even if it was as part of the strategic planning team.

He clambered from his vehicle with all the grace of a three-legged giraffe. Bloody good thing none of the top brass were witnesses. He'd hate getting stood down on medical grounds. Too much time to think about other parts of his life.

Laura and the baby.

Summer.

Nikolai unlocked the door and dragged his weary bones inside. With the house locked all day, the scent of paint fumes almost knocked him over. And that sent his thoughts winging to Summer. He'd come to a decision. He had to stop seeing her in any capacity, except as a neighbor. Horizontal dancing was a no-go.

He scrubbed his hands over his stubbled jaw. His smell offended him, but hell, he needed a drink before a shower. He hobbled into the kitchen, opened a window and pulled out a bottle of whiskey from the pantry. Irish whiskey that was too good to gulp as he intended.

Nikolai grabbed a glass and made it as far as the table before a jagged shard of pain had him cursing. He sank into a chair and slumped to ride out the agonizing waves targeting his knee. Shit, he'd been okay this morning. He hoped like hell his injury settled in time for another go-round.

He leaned back in the wooden chair, knowing he needed to take it easy on the alcohol despite his driving need to bury painful memories. He let the whiskey burn down his throat in a slow trickle.

Outside, darkness approached despite the extra hour of light granted by daylight saving. The faint call of a seabird drifted on the breeze. A soft creak made

Nikolai's hand clench around the glass. Shit. He watched as she closed the small gate connecting the two properties. She skipped across the lawn, her blue hair fanning out behind her.

Even though he knew he'd have to blow her off, his heart skipped a beat. She wouldn't make this easy for him. He knew it at gut level.

"Pooh! It stinks of paint in here," she called from the front door.

"Wait until you get a whiff of me."

She appeared in the doorway, fingers holding her nose, blue eyes wide and twinkling. "What have you been doing?"

"Training with the men for a mission."

"What about your knee?"

"My knee is fine." Hell, maybe if he said it enough it might come true. As if he didn't have enough worry bones to gnaw.

"Good." Summer seemed unperturbed by his temper.

Nikolai wondered about her reaction when he told her they couldn't be together anymore. Their relationship was a mistake—a slip of judgment on his part.

He hoped like hell she didn't cry. The way he was feeling, he might just break out and howl with her. He took another sip of whiskey and savored the burn as it slid down his throat.

"Are you going to have a shower? I could scrub your back."

"I thought the paint bothered you."

"It does, but I came prepared." She dug inside a pocket and brandished an inhaler for him to see.

Fuck, she wasn't gonna make it easy. Nikolai stared at the dregs of amber liquid in his glass. Maybe he should lay out the truth, tell her why he was bad relationship material. His gut twisted at laying his emotions bare.

He cleared his throat. "Henry won't approve of us having a relationship."

Summer straightened from her sprawl against the doorframe and crossed her arms, her chin angled in challenge. "Uncle Henry isn't here. And even if he was, it's none of his business. I'm legal."

"He asked me to look after you, not to drag you off to bed and fuck you." Nikolai let gritty harshness fill his voice, made himself sound tough. Inside, he felt like crap.

"My mother isn't here. You can say that word, you know. I have heard it before."

"Summer." He wanted to shake her. He wanted to kiss her. But he wasn't fool enough to reach for her.

"I'm going out to a nightclub on

Friday night. The new one—Raven Black. You—"

He cursed and slammed his glass on the table hard enough to make her jump.

"Who are you going with?" Jealousy, pure and simple, poured out with his words. Fuck, was that a giveaway or what?

"With some of the girls from work."

"It's not safe." He'd heard about the Raven Black. All sorts of kinky things... Jake and Louie had picked up a couple of women there... "You're not going unless I go too."

"And are you going as my boyfriend or my chaperone?"

"Dammit, this isn't funny. I'm bad news."

"So you keep saying." She advanced to his table and jerked out a chair. She sat and faced him in clear expectation. "Tell me why. Let me judge."

"It won't change anything."

Obviously not the best time to tell him about exchanging the books, or the prickling instinct she experienced whenever she left the house. She took a shallow breath and ended up with a lungful of paint fumes. Standing abruptly, she stood and dragged her chair over to the open window before sitting again.

"So, tell me about this bad thing you've done. Do a proper job and scare me off." Her tone was mocking but inside, panic jumped with the vigor of a kangaroo. She liked Nikolai, and despite his alpha gene, they were good together. Given time, she might even cure him of the bossiness.

Anguish crossed his face briefly before

his expression blanked. He snatched the bottle of whiskey and poured some into his glass. Then he glanced at her with chocolate-brown eyes full of pain and tortured memories. "Want some?"

"Sure, why not?" She jumped up to get a glass and moved her chair next to him. He poured her a drink, and she waited for him to speak. He glanced at her, hesitated. His broad chest rose and fell before he averted his attention.

"I was married before," he said, concentrating on his glass.

Summer caught her breath. He was older. Of course, he'd had relationships with other women. But it still hurt, dammit.

"Laura and I married young."

Bother. Now the woman had a name. Summer bet she was slim, blonde and beautiful. Everything she wasn't.

"We married too young. Neither of us... We shouldn't have wed, but Laura had problems with her father. He was a drunk, and he used to bash anyone who got in his way. Marriage seemed like the best solution. I mean, we'd known each other since we were kids."

Summer's mind raced. What had happened to Laura? Why weren't they together now? Questions pounded her mind while she waited for him to speak again. "And?"

"The marriage didn't work out."

Duh! She wanted to give him a good shake. Now was not the time to turn taciturn. "Why didn't it work out?"

"We married too young. I was away a lot for work. Laura was bored."

"Why didn't she get a job? It wasn't your fault she had too much time on her hands."

Nikolai's head jerked up. He stared at her as though she'd suddenly sprouted another head. "Is that what you would have done?" His tone was harsh, his face tormented like a man in the grip of deep emotions.

Summer was confused. Wasn't a job the obvious solution? Or volunteer work? Or some sort of hobby? It was what she would have done in the same situation. The world was full of new things to learn, new things to experience like the bungee off the top of the Sky Tower in central Auckland, which Summer had booked, along with some of the girls at the library. Next week was D-day, and she was already scared spitless. But fear wasn't going to stop her grabbing a new experience.

"Boredom and the need for change was one of the reasons I jumped at the chance to do the library course in Auckland. Eketahuna is a small town with not much social life. Everyone knows me there."

"You mean you can't get up to mischief there."

"True. That and the fact most of the eligible males my age are too frightened of my brothers to ask me out." She scrutinized Nikolai. Calmer now, not so introspective, but that didn't mean she intended to let him change the subject. He owed her an explanation. And once she had it, she intended to entice him into bed. Actually, make that shower first and bed second. The man didn't smell pretty.

"Laura was bored. She met up with some old school friends while I was away on a mission. She wrote and told me about it. I was pleased because she sounded happier. It made things easier when I managed a few weeks at home." Nikolai paused again and seemed to drift off.

"Nikolai," she said, reaching over to pat his arm. "Tell me, before I'm too old and gray to sympathize."

He speared her with a narrow-eyed glare. "The group she hooked up with was into drugs. Anything they could get. Ecstasy. P. Among others."

"I'm sorry, Nikolai." She squeezed his biceps in a show of sympathy. "But you can't blame yourself because she took drugs. We all have freedom of choice."

"But I left her alone. I thought she'd kicked the habit. She went to rehab and came home clean. We were expecting our first child."

A lump the size of a golf ball clogged her throat. She swallowed several times, but her throat remained tight and tears of sympathy prickled at the back of her eyes. A child. That made Laura more real—an image that was harder to fight. "What happened?"

"I'd gone off on a mission. Communication back home was difficult. I'd talked to Laura on the phone a couple of times, and she sounded happy. The mission was extended. Something happened. I'm not sure what set her off, but she started doing drugs again. The police told me her system was full of P. She drove off a ravine on the way home."

Despite squeezing her eyes shut, a tear escaped and trickled down her cheek.

"Don't cry, dammit," Nikolai snarled. "I know I screwed up. I should never have left her alone. Now you know why any sort of relationship between us is impossible. I have a demanding job. I can't guarantee I'd be here when you need me."

Summer swiped at the tears on her face with her hand. Resentment burned in her gut. Who'd asked him to babysit her anyway? Everyone kept forgetting she was an adult, and it was time for them to remember. She jerked upright, standing rigidly to attention. "I don't need a babysitter. What I need, what I want, is a lover. I thought you were my lover. Obviously, I was wrong." She stormed to the door and took great pleasure in slamming the door on the way out.

Chapter 14

The impact of wood against frame reverberated like thunder, and Nikolai could have sworn the house shuddered.

He'd done it.

He'd driven off Summer.

So why didn't he feel good about returning to the friends-and-neighbor slot? Because he—

Damn! He wasn't gonna think about entering emotional territory. That was what tripped him every bloody time. No point repeating mistakes.

He hauled his body off the chair and limped to the kitchen doorway. His progress to his bedroom was slow and laborious, his boots leaving a trail of dried mud as witness to his journey. He'd clean up when he had more energy. The reality of failing to tackle the assault course tomorrow darted to mind, but he shied from the possibility and continued his journey to his bedroom. Once there, he dropped to the bed with a pained groan to remove his boots. More caked mud dropped onto the gleaming wooden floor he'd rescued from under a layer of brown carpet.

His thoughts wandered back to Summer, and the look on her face right before she stormed from his house. He'd hurt her just as he'd distressed Laura with his frequent absences. Trouble was, he loved his job and wasn't trained for anything else.

"Get over it, Tarei." He yanked off his shirt and struggled from his army fatigue trousers. The deed was done. Summer and he were no longer an item, and that was the way he wanted it.

Summer hadn't spoken to Nikolai for three days. She rose at the ring of the alarm clock each morning, dragged her weary body from bed and went to work. The days passed like the slow trickle of syrup on a winter's day. Despite trying to keep busy, her mind kept wandering back to Nikolai and the pleasure they'd experienced together.

Her mouth firmed as she watched him limp from his house and climb into a battered sedan driven by his mate, Jake.

Stubborn, infuriating male.

She glared through the closed window, confident in the knowledge he wouldn't know she was spying. The limp had returned. He shouldn't try to work at present or he'd end up with a permanent hobble. The scar that sliced past his kneecap signified the extent of the damage.

The man needed a keeper.

A babysitter.

Ten minutes later, she rushed out the door and locked it before heading for her Mazda. It was good to have the old girl back from the garage. She checked her watch, let out a yelp and ran the remaining distance to her car.

Luck was with her as the traffic was lighter than normal on the run up the motorway to central Auckland. She rushed into the staff meeting room at two minutes to the hour.

"Just made it," Angel said.

Summer slid into the empty chair beside her friend and attempted composure.

"Give up," Angel said. "Your cheeks are scarlet, your hair has gone wispy and you're breathing like a dragon about to put out a fire."

"Charming," she muttered. "With friends like you—"

"Have you heard about the...?"

Summer listened with half an ear, as she sometimes did with Angel. Although she liked her and found her fun to work with, Angel loved to gossip. Which was why she hadn't mentioned Nikolai to her friend. She didn't want her personal life all over the library.

"Summer." Angel shook her, digging her lilac-tipped nails into Summer's upper arm. "The murder at the bookshop. Have you heard about it?"

Summer shot to attention. "Murder?"

A fine tremor shook the hand that rested on the desktop. She snatched it off the wooden surface and stuck it on her lap out of sight. Thoughts screamed through her mind fast as boy-racers and their cars on a Friday night.

"Where?" she demanded, a sharp edge to her voice.

Rapid footsteps outside the meeting room heralded Mrs. Ferguson's arrival. She bustled into the room, casting an eagle eye over her charges. "Good, everyone's here. We have a lot to get through."

"Which bookshop?" Summer mouthed urgently at Angel.

"Summer Williams." Mrs. Ferguson's voice cut across the hushed silence. "Organize your social life during your lunch hour."

"Sorry, Mrs. Ferguson," she said, working at maintaining a calm façade. Difficult when worry, fear and outright panic stampeded through her brain.

What had she done?

"Firstly, I'd like to talk about the training courses..."

Summer tuned her boss out while her mind dwelled on murder. Although Angel hadn't confirmed the whom, she didn't believe in coincidences, not since she'd swapped the books.

Lord, what was she going to do? Panic swarmed through her stomach like a malignant virus. Her lungs tightened so much it felt as if she were pushing weights off her chest with each breath. She bent to fumble through her handbag for her inhaler and took a quick, furtive puff.

"Summer!"

Summer jerked upward and hit her head on the corner of the wooden table as she straightened in her chair. Pain lanced through her head, and she bit back a groan. Bother. Another knock to the noggin. Just the thing for clear thinking.

"What are you doing?" Mrs. Ferguson glared at her across the top of her rimless glasses.

Summer bit her lip, while tears smarted at the corners of her eyes. Her fingers delicately probed the tender spot. Great. Another lump on her head to match the previous one. "I'm sorry. My asthma is giving me trouble. I needed to use my inhaler."

The harsh expression on Mrs. Ferguson's face faded to concern. "Do you need to leave the room for a few minutes?"

"I think I'll be okay. I'm sorry for interrupting."

Mrs. Ferguson continued, and she tried

to concentrate. But it was difficult when guilt coursed through her. She couldn't help but wonder if the murder had happened because of her actions.

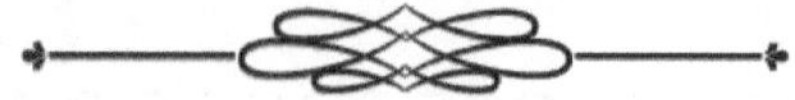

Summer hadn't made a conscious decision to tell Nikolai, but she found herself looking for him while watering Uncle Henry's roses. She aimed the hose at the base of Tom Thumb, Uncle Henry's favorite, and tried to quell the ever-present anxiety.

The weird thing was Dare hadn't rung to ask about the book. If he'd found something wrong, wouldn't he have contacted her? Apart from a hurried phone call, canceling a dinner date, she hadn't heard from him.

He hadn't mentioned the book.

After soaking the roses for way too

long, Nikolai still hadn't arrived home. Summer weeded the garden, a chore she hated, and mowed the lawn. Still, the man hadn't returned.

Darkness crept over the landscape, cloaking the trees and paddocks with the same murky gray. Birds fell silent and drivers on the country road switched on their headlights.

Still no Nikolai.

She wandered inside and flicked on a light. After toeing off her red canvas shoes, she headed for the kitchen. Halfway along the passage, she paused and turned back to lock the door.

The strident ring of the phone pulled her from thoughts of murder.

"Hello."

"Hello, Summer."

"Who is this?" The hoarse whisper brought a rash of goose bumps. The fact that the man—whoever he was—knew her name sent terror skittering on the heels of the goose bumps.

"Watch your back, girlie."

"Who is this? If you don't stop, I'll—"

The phone thumped down on the other end, leaving her talking to herself. Swallowing, she replaced the phone. There had been several heavy breathing calls. This was the first time her caller had spoken.

Summer glanced out the kitchen window. What if Nikolai wasn't coming home tonight?

Although she was tired of orders from her family and Nikolai, there was the odd time when their bossiness felt right.

Even confiding her fears would help. She picked up the newspaper she'd purchased during her lunch hour. Not that it had given many details of the murder.

> Man Found Dead in Bookshop.
> The owner of the Pen and
> Quill bookshop was found in
> the early hours of Wednesday
> morning. Police suspect theft
> was the motive and are chasing
> up several leads.

Summer dropped the Herald back onto the bench top with a sigh. Theft, they said. But what if it hadn't been theft? What if murder was the motive, and the culprits had made it look like a burglary to throw the police off the trail?

The faint sound of a car pierced her troubled mind. She ran for the window. The vehicle slowed, its headlights piercing the darkness and highlighting the hedge that ran the length of the roadside boundary.

It wasn't Nikolai.

Summer stilled before she realized with the light on in the kitchen and the curtains and blinds wide open, anyone would be able to see inside the house. Ducking out of sight, she leapt for the light switch and flipped it off. It took precious seconds for her eyes to adjust to the dark, and by the time she reached the window, the headlights were no longer visible.

The car was gone.

Or was it?

Her stomach knotted, her imagination conjuring dragons and monsters lurking in the dark. She peered into the front garden and scrutinized the shadows.

Nothing.

But that didn't mean a thing.

Uncle Henry had so many bushes

and hedges in his flourishing garden. Anyone with nefarious purposes could hide or skulk close to the house without detection.

A sharp creak sounded.

Shit. Had she shut the gate between the property boundaries after visiting Nikolai earlier? Or had someone else left the catch unfastened?

She licked her lips as she tried to remember. The sound repeated. A ghostly rat-tat-tat. Summer clasped and unclasped sweaty palms. Overactive imagination. That was what she hoped.

Voices drifted in the air and a vehicle engine fired to life. Light flooded the area behind the hedge, and it bled through the greenery to her side, casting huge black shadows. The car drove away and some of the tension bled from her tense limbs. The driver had probably stopped to answer his cell phone or for some equally innocent reason.

She expelled a breath. Telling herself to quit the drama queen act, she made her way to her bedroom and started preparations for bed. She was about to climb into bed when she decided it would be a good idea to have her phone handy. She switched on the passage light and when she saw it was clear, ran into the kitchen, scooped up the phone and tore back to bed.

"Get a grip, Summer." The sound of her voice didn't offer comfort. It just made her isolation feel more real.

The phone rang again. Summer started, and a gasp escaped before she could bite it back. The sharp peal of the phone continued. She needed to answer in case it was Uncle Henry. With a shaky hand, she stabbed the answer button and held it to her ear.

"Hello."

"That you, Mariah?" The deep masculine voice sent ripples of apprehension writhing like snakes.

She jerked upright in bed. "I think you have the wrong number."

"Don't think so. It's right here on the telephone booth. Mariah Twining will jump-start your day."

"No, I—"

"How much you charge for extras? You do extras dontcha?"

Summer hung up. Almost immediately, the phone rang again. Uncle Henry had rung a few nights ago. It was improbable he'd call again in the same week.

She turned off the phone, closed her eyes and tried to ignore the empty sound of the night...

Suddenly, she jerked awake. The crick

in her neck told her she'd fallen asleep with her neck at a weird angle. Tension seeped through her, the silence in her dark room broken by the tick of her alarm clock. She strained her ears for anything out of the ordinary.

When nothing sounded out of place, she fumbled for the bedside lamp. Almost one in the morning. Surely, Nikolai would be home by now.

She reached for her phone and jerked her hand back. Ringing him was admitting she required help because of this mess.

"Stop being stupid. You can't carry on like this."

Biting her lip, she reached for the phone and punched the speed dial button for Nikolai.

"Yeah?"

"It's me. Summer."

"What is it?" He sounded alert—a good man to have in her corner.

"Can... Could you come over?" The last of her words rushed out so quickly they tangled on her tongue. Asking for help sent a quiver of anxiety through her too. What if he turned around and told her uncle? Uncle Henry would feel obliged to ring her parents. It would be like a chain reaction if she didn't handle things with speed and decisiveness.

"Now?"

"Yes, please," she whispered.

"Make coffee. I'll be there in five." The phone crashed down on his end.

Summer pulled a face and saluted with her free hand. "Yes, sir." She placed the phone on the bedside table and dressed. The idea of meeting Nikolai in her nightie made her feel weird, even though he'd seen her naked. A knock sounded on the door as she plugged in the coffeemaker.

"What is it?" Nikolai demanded, pushing past her.

Summer stared at him wordlessly, her body responding to his nearness even more now that she knew what it felt like to touch his skin and run her fingers across his muscles. His dark hair was a wild jumble of damp curls that made her palms itch to touch. His jeans hugged his hips, his muscular thighs and no doubt his butt if he'd taken the time to do a twirl. He hadn't bothered to don a shirt, and his hairless chest rose and fell with each breath.

"If you've finished undressing me, maybe you could get to the point."

Had she made a mistake? Maybe she should've called home.

"Summer, I haven't slept for hours.

Please spit out whatever you need to say then I can get some sleep. Did you make coffee?"

"It's almost ready." She shut the front door and walked past him, careful not to touch while passing.

As she led the way to the kitchen, she felt his gaze. A tingle of excitement sprang to life inside despite the harsh words between them. Lord, she missed him. She'd tried to tell herself she could get by without him, but the truth—the truth was she wanted to jump his bones. More than that, she wanted an exclusive relationship. But that wasn't going to happen, not when he insisted on living in the shadows of the past.

In the kitchen, Summer poured coffee. All the time, she was aware of his enigmatic gaze, his scent of raw male and soap, and the sounds he made as he settled onto a stool at the breakfast bar.

She hesitated. Where to start? At the beginning. Yes, the beginning.

"I met Dare because somehow I received his book special order instead of mine."

"That's how you met the clotheshorse?" His brow wrinkled as she handed him a mug of coffee. "How did you know they were his books?"

"The order had a card inside. I went to the address, and that's when I met him. We exchanged packages and went from there."

A low growl vibrated in the air between them. "And?"

"Maybe this isn't such a good idea."

"Summer." Nikolai placed his mug on the breakfast bar with a soft clunk. He prowled toward her.

She found herself backing up until the

kitchen cabinets blocked her retreat. Seconds later, Nikolai's hands thumped either side of her, effectively caging her in place. She swallowed.

"Spit out your problem. I don't have time for games."

"Since I frequent the bookshop often, I've picked up the odd package for him. Last week, I brought Dare's books home. We were going to go out for dinner, but he had to cancel because a business contact wanted a meeting."

Nikolai's jaw clenched. "I told you the man was bad news."

Her mood veered sharply to anger. "Look, this is hard enough without you saying 'I told you so'."

He gave a clipped nod but didn't move. Having his bulk so close made her nervous. Actually, that wasn't quite the truth. He made her think of sex—sweaty bodies sliding together in a sensual dance. Her body. His body.

Summer swallowed convulsively and felt the inevitable heat swamp her face. She hurried into speech to hide her unease at his proximity.

"I don't know why, but I opened the package. It was the same title as the first book. A book on fly-fishing."

"Fly-fishing." Nikolai expressed his opinion with a sharp snort. "Hard to believe the clotheshorse likes standing up to his waist in icy mountain water."

Summer agreed but didn't comment. "It made me think. I couldn't believe Dare would buy a book for one of his brothers or his father. They didn't strike me as fishermen either. The more I thought about it, the weirder it seemed. So, I found another fly-fishing book and replaced it, and yesterday the owner of the bookshop was found murdered in his shop."

"You did what?" Nikolai's tempered voice was far worse than a bellow.

"I exchanged the books," she whispered. "I think it's my fault the man was murdered."

"Fuck." Nikolai moved without warning, stalking across the kitchen floor with a distinct hitch in his stride. "What did you do with the book?"

"It's in my room."

"You'd better get it."

"But there's nothing different about it. I've checked."

"Let me look. Another set of eyes."

Nikolai watched the sway of her hips as she hurried away to get the book. The urgent need to throw her over his shoulder and lock her away somewhere safe pounded through him. The situation she described stunk to high heavens, his senses screeching danger.

Summer appeared minutes later with the book and handed it to him. Fly-Fishing in New Zealand. He checked the book. Nothing seemed out of the ordinary, yet like Summer, his gut screamed there was something odd.

He placed the book on the table between them and noticed Summer stared at it as though it were a rabid rat, poised to leap on her and nip. "What do you know about the murder?"

"There wasn't much in the Herald." She stood, picked up a paper off the kitchen counter, and after scanning the first few pages, handed it to him.

Nikolai read it and glanced at Summer. Her face was pale with a fine dusting of freckles visible on the bridge of her nose and cheeks. His gut twisted. She was intelligent enough to know she was in danger.

He knew it too.

"You can't stay here alone." He captured her face in his hand and gently forced her to meet his gaze. "I know you value your independence, but it's too dangerous for you here on your own. If Dare's involved, and we have to assume he is, he'll be eliminating every possibility. You'll be on that list."

He saw her swallow once and then again. "I know. Nikolai, what should I do?"

The underlying terror in her voice tugged at him. Responsibility sat uneasily on his shoulders as he shuffled through possible solutions. Hell, what if he screwed up again?

He shoved the thought aside. He'd do what he did on a mission, what he was trained to do—plan objective. Carry out objective.

"I think one of Jake's brothers is based at Auckland Central. I'll start things rolling. I want you to pack a bag. You'll have to stay with me." And he'd have to try to keep his hands to himself.

He glanced at her, his cock sitting up with clear expectation, pressing against his zipper until he had to make a clandestine move for comfort. Yeah, no problem—as long as she reverted to her sack dresses he'd have no problems at all.

"Nikolai, I know it makes sense not to stay here, but I can't stay at your house."

"Why not?" The rejection stung. "Don't you trust me?"

Summer came to him then and before

he could blink, plopped on his lap. His arms came around her automatically, and it was like coming home—her flowery scent, her soft feminine curves, her butt rubbing against his militant cock.

He closed his eyes briefly and fought to remember the dangerous situation Summer was in. She needed a friend right now, not a lover. But couldn't he be both?

"My asthma is acting up lately. I don't want to risk the paint smell setting off an attack. It would make me even more vulnerable."

"Okay. Pack a bag. We'll go to Jake's and cadge a room there."

"What about the book?"

"We'll take it with us. I'll wait for you then grab a few things from my place."

Summer nodded and climbed off his

knee. He wanted to protest her leaving and grab her back. But he did neither.

His mission was to keep her safe, and that was all.

Chapter 15

Jake's house was in Red Hill, a short drive away. Nikolai drove his four-wheel drive vehicle via a circuitous route, which took an extra ten minutes, but by the time they arrived, he was positive no one had followed them.

The porch light was on when they pulled up, and the front door flew open. A sleepy-looking Jake ushered them inside and locked the door after them.

"Thanks," Nikolai said.

"No problem, man. Spare room is through there. You know where everything is. I'm going back to bed." Jake yawned, scratched his bare chest, and wandered off, disappearing down a dark passageway.

"Come on. I'll show you the spare room." Nikolai flipped on a light and ushered her into a double room. The bed dominated the space, diverting his worries from crime bosses to a more direct problem—keeping his hands to himself.

He halted, unwilling to step farther inside.

"Bathroom and toilet are right next door." Nikolai scanned her pale face and knew she needed sleep. "If you don't need anything else, I'll leave you to get some sleep."

"Nikolai." Her soft voice froze him to the spot. "I don't want to sleep alone. Please stay with me."

If she had flirted or tried to seduce him, he wouldn't have had any trouble saying no. He was used to knocking aside military groupies. But the unwilling plea in her voice drew him closer. "I'll stay with you until you go to sleep."

She bit her bottom lip and rushed into speech. "The bed's big enough for both of us. Stay."

Hell, it was what he wanted, wasn't it? To watch over her. He could do it easily here in the same room.

"Sleep. Nothing else," he said, spelling it out while inside he railed at the impossibility of a relationship between them.

Summer nodded and pulled out an oversized T-shirt from her overnight bag. She turned her back, stripped and tugged the pale blue T-shirt over her head. When she pulled back the bed covers, he was still staring.

He jerked from his reverie, and immediately another problem

presented itself. He hadn't packed clothes. His eyes zapped to Summer.

"I know I'm safe with you. You've made it very clear you don't want a relationship with me, but I thought we were friends. I've seen your body before. I don't want anything other than friendly comfort." Her gorgeous mouth twisted. "I won't push in where I'm not wanted."

She climbed beneath the covers and turned her back to him as though she didn't care.

God, he wanted to stay even though he knew it wasn't wise. He consciously relaxed his tense shoulders and took the weight off his aching knee. His inability to protect the ones he loved lay at the root of his confusion. He acknowledged that. His hands went to the button fly on his jeans. Then he yanked his shirt over his head and discarded it. Seconds later, his shoes and the rest of his clothes joined his T-shirt on the floor, and he flicked off the light then slid into bed.

"Thanks."

The soft whisper warmed him and steeled his willpower. She required comfort and protection. He could try to give that to the best of his ability. He moved closer until he was almost touching her. Gradually the tautness dissolved from his muscles. Summer's slow, deep breaths told him she'd dropped off to sleep. The best thing for her. He'd noticed her weight loss. Knowing they were safe tonight, at least, he closed his eyes and let sleep take him.

Nikolai jerked awake. His heart slammed in an adrenaline rush before he calmed enough to realize he'd drifted into a nightmare. The vision of Laura floated through his mind again without warning, followed by one of the young soldiers who'd lost his life on the same mission in which he'd injured his knee.

Both glared at him through reproachful eyes. A bad omen? He wasn't sure, but he knew he wouldn't rest easy until Dare Martin was behind bars, and Summer was home in Eketahuna, safe in the care of her family. Yeah. He'd rest much easier once he'd handed over his responsibility.

Warm water bubbled around Summer's bare shoulders the next day. In a flax bush over to her right, a pair of tuis squabbled over the nectar from a spear-like flower head. A third tui flew in to join the pair and a noisy fight ensued. Gradually, one bird emerged the victor and peace reigned again as it fed. Jake's garden, at the rear of his house, was a private haven and perfect for her current mood.

She stretched, languid and indolent, her muscles relaxing as the warm water in the spa pummeled them. She closed her eyes and lay there in lazy enjoyment.

What was she going to do about Nikolai?

They'd woken this morning with limbs entwined, his morning erection nestling against her belly. It would have been so easy to lift her hips and join their bodies. She'd wanted to carry out the thought. Desperately.

But something had kept her from the overt action. Nikolai had to make the first move. While he mightn't have objected, later he'd have second thoughts. She needed the skill and patience of a fly-fisher to hook the big, bad SAS man, because if there was one thing she'd learned in the last twelve hours, it was that she wanted Nikolai.

These last few days without him had made her plain miserable.

A splash jerked her eyes open in sudden fear. She jerked upright. Her pulse leveled out again when she recognized Nikolai sitting on the opposite side of the spa pool.

"Sorry. Didn't mean to frighten you. I should have called out." His eyes narrowed and a frown appeared. "You're naked."

Give the man a prize. Her pulse accelerated again, and it had nothing to do with fear. "Jake said he wouldn't be home until late. I assumed you'd be back the same time." She relaxed against the edge of the spa and casually allowed a nipple to peek from beneath the layer of bubbles. The combination of cooler air and the plain naughtiness of her actions drew her nipple tight. A corresponding jump low in her belly made anticipation leap to life.

Nikolai didn't take his eyes off her. The spa and the peaceful garden didn't relax his tense shoulders. She bit back the need to laugh. Interesting. What could she do next? The pleasant buzz spread downward into her pussy.

"Thank you for last night," she said.

"I can't hear."

Good. Impish laughter tickled her insides. She'd have to move closer.

"Ah, Summer. Stay there." He sounded distinctly rattled.

Excellent. She pretended she didn't hear and shot across the spa pool to the molded seat right next to him. She allowed her arm and thigh to trespass into his space. Seduction sounded like a damn fine idea. Her body craved him. She plain wanted him. They were consenting adults.

No problem.

"How is your knee?"

"The medical people have told me to take off another two weeks," Nikolai said in clear disgust.

"You shouldn't have overdone it."

"Don't nag."

"Fine." She sidled closer and allowed both breasts to peek from the water. Encouraged by his obvious interest, she stretched, arms rising into the air.

"Thank you for helping me last night."

"No problem."

"Kiss me, Nikolai."

"Not a good idea." He ripped his gaze from her breasts.

"Why not?"

"You know why not."

Frustration made her testy. Irritation zapped through her, wanting an outlet, needing a vent.

"I need sexual release," she said. "If you're not interested, I'll use a toy." She stood, hoping for a reaction because if he called her bluff, she had no idea what to try next. "Or maybe one of the spa jets would do the job."

She studied him through lowered lashes. He wasn't moving. Bother. Epic fail. She turned to climb from the pool, lifting her legs and brazenly flashing her feminine folds as she stepped from the spa.

"Wait." He grabbed her arm and jerked her to a halt. She toppled off balance, but he caught her and dragged her into the safety of his arms. "I can make you climax."

"You sure can," she purred. "And are you going to or are you all talk?"

Nikolai snorted right next to her ear. "Stop trying to push. If I decide to fuck you, I'll do it in my own good time. Not when you think I should."

His breath brushed across her ear and the tender skin of her neck. She had the man on a hook—he just didn't like to admit defeat.

"So are we going to make love, or do I need to get that toy?" She didn't bother telling him the toy was still in its original packaging.

Nikolai drew away far enough to see her eyes. "Baggage." Humor lit his chocolate-brown gaze, and she knew everything would turn out all right.

Her body reacted swiftly, the slow burn of pleasure igniting with his attention.

"This thing between us—it won't last. It

can't."

Still fighting. Still thinking he knew what would be best for her. Oh, well. They had plenty of time until she returned to Eketahuna. She'd wear down his objections one by one. She wriggled around until she straddled his legs. He still wore underwear, but it wasn't difficult to gauge his interest. All she needed was time.

His eyes dropped to her breasts, the sensation of his gaze wandering her curves sending tendrils of pleasure fizzing through her. Teasing, she cupped one breast in her hands and offered it to him.

"Taste me," she whispered. "Make me feel good."

"You'd tempt a saint."

"You're not a saint. And why would you want to be? I'd think someone who acts pure all the time misses out on a lot of fun. Go on, Nikolai. Taste me."

He lowered his head and licked her distended nipple. "Any other instructions?" He nipped the fleshy underside before he licked a wet path down her cleavage. His mouth alternated between breasts, sucking, and laving until she whimpered with enjoyment.

"No more instructions," she gasped out. "You have more experience. I'm willing to go with the flow."

He snorted a laugh but at least he started to cooperate. With his mouth surrounding her nipple, warmth bloomed between her legs. Each draw of his mouth, each kiss sent a bolt of sensation to her core. She squirmed closer until her pussy brushed the hard bulge at his groin. The spasm of flickering response from her clit had her gasping, grabbing his shoulders for purchase. She threw back her head and rotated her hips, so his boxer-covered erection brushed her clit again.

Without warning, he surged to his feet. She squeaked, thinking he'd drop her, but he held her easily without even breathing hard. While she clutched at his neck and had her legs hooked around his waist, Nikolai yanked his boxers down and stepped out of them. Then he sat again, strumming his thumbs over both nipples and staring straight into her eyes.

She leaned closer and brushed her lips across his. A teasing kiss flared hot and serious. Tongues stroked and dueled as she squirmed closer. Even though it had only been a few days, hunger gnawed at her mind, her body. She strained upward, seeking a way to ease the sexual tension gripping her body.

The warm pulse of the spa jets intensified the craving, the hunger, the desperate need to join with him. His cock brushed against her but not where she needed him most. Just a fraction to the left. She slipped her hand between them and brushed her thumb over his tip. His eyes dropped to half-mast and a distinct shudder ripped through him.

"I've missed you," he murmured. "I tried not to."

She took pleasure from his raw honesty and stretched upward to reward him with a lingering kiss, the slow slide of his tongue against hers building the excitement. She leaned closer, brushing her breasts against his smooth chest, reveling in the drag of friction.

"Ohhh," she groaned. The frisson of pleasure felt good but not as satisfying as Nikolai's cock. Without thinking, she guided his cock to her pussy mouth and sank down. He was wide. Thick. So good as she stretched around him, taking him inside her channel. She lifted her hips and sank back down, setting an instinctive rhythm.

The powerful thrust of his body when he surged upward sent desire flowing like honey. And it was just as sweet.

"Fuck." Nikolai grasped her hips and wrenched his cock from her.

"What are you—?"

"No condom." His chest rose and fell rapidly as though he'd run a race. "Shit, I can't believe that just happened. What was I thinking?" He swept his wet hair away from his face and met her frown unflinching. "That's it. We'll get married."

Summer gaped at him, certain she hadn't misheard.

"No. I don't think so." She scrambled off his lap and stood, darting out of reach when he tried to snare her hand. With more haste than dignity, she climbed from the spa. "I'll go and get a condom. I brought some with me. Won't be long."

"Summer." The low masculine growl spurred her to speed.

What was wrong with him? Most men thought with their dicks or at least ceased rational thought when their cocks were involved. But not the big, bad SAS man. Oh, no!

He had to be the voice of reason.

She ignored the chatter at the back of her head that said she was acting like a child, the one that said Nikolai was acting responsibly. As he should.

"Dammit, Summer. Come back here."

Summer heard the splash of water and rapid footsteps across the wooden deck. She increased her speed while her anger grew. Pompous man! How dare he try to order her around?

She refused to marry him.

"Summer." A hand closed over her bare shoulder before she made it halfway down the passage, whirling her around to face him. "What's your problem? I thought females wanted marriage."

"They like to be asked," she snapped.

His dark brows furrowed. "So, I'll ask. Will you marry me?"

Fury, hot and savage, curled her hands to fists. If he uttered one more word, she'd deck him—right in the middle of his perfectly straight nose. "No. No, I will not marry you. All I want from you is a good, fun fuck. Is that plain enough? You told me before you didn't want responsibility. Fine. I'm taking you at your word. I don't want responsibility either."

"What if you're pregnant?"

"We're talking if." Summer felt as if he'd stabbed her through the heart. Thoughts whirred and tangled in one confused mass. Not that she intended to scrutinize them too closely.

Nikolai didn't want marriage, and he'd proposed because the thought of failing another child ate at him. If she got married, when she married, she wanted to know she was loved.

Cherished.

The idea of Nikolai considering her a duty left her cold. Her nose rose in the air. "I'm twenty-two. That's too young to get married. You said yourself I'm too young for you. And here I thought women were the indecisive ones." She jerked open the door of their allocated bedroom and stomped inside with Nikolai a step behind.

Cold fear kicked him in the gut, but despite the terror, he could still appreciate a great arse when he saw one. Tight and round, it begged for fondling. He watched her bend over and flash the pink folds of her labia at him. Then she whirled about and slapped a small foil package in his hand.

"Now, can we have sex?" she demanded.

Her beautiful breasts rose and fell, distracting him for an instant. His eyes narrowed as he studied her flushed cheeks and swollen lips. The woman was marrying him if he had to drag her to a justice of the peace.

While Nikolai debated his course of

action, he peered at the condom wrapper. "Chocolate flavored. What happened to the glow-in-the-dark green?"

"I thought a change would be nice." Summer sat on the edge of the bed and primly crossed her legs.

Nikolai handed the foil package back to her. He wasn't averse to sex, as his rampant penis indicated, but come hell, high water or local crooks, she would become Mrs. Tarei.

"You put it on." He dropped onto the mattress, calmly folded his arms across his chest to wait. A smirk built, just bursting to break out as he watched her hesitate.

"I've never done it before. Apart from the banana, and I suppose that doesn't count. Fruit isn't quite as distracting."

"It's not difficult. If you want a bout of

sweaty sex, you're gonna have to learn in a hurry."

"All right." She bounced to her feet, the abrupt move sending her ripe, luscious breasts swaying gently. Acute anticipation quickened his pulse rate as she turned away and bent to rifle through her bag. She pulled out the box of condoms. For a puzzled second Nikolai stared, then he got the picture. Summer was a librarian, trained to look up books, so if she wanted to learn a new skill, she read about it. Her pink lips moved as she mouthed the instructions and studied the diagrams on the enclosed leaflet. "Okay. Refresher done. I've got this sussed. I know what I'm doing."

A chuckle burst from him. "Do your worst."

She tore open the wrapping, used her

thumb to hold the end, and rolled it on as though she'd been applying condoms to men's cocks for years. "Ta da!"

Her flush of achievement made him want to chuckle. He wondered if she would attack parenthood with the same single-minded determination. "Come here," he said.

"At last." Summer wrinkled her nose. "Some action."

Nikolai lurched for her, grabbing and twisting her body so she fell flat on the mattress beneath him. He stared down into her flushed face. Hell, she aroused him without even trying. He bent his head, licking a few remaining droplets of water from the spa off her collarbone. Then he moved down her body to pay homage to her full breasts, drawing circles across the pale globes with his tongue.

She tried to direct his mouth to her nipple by entwining her fingers in his hair and tugging. Instead, he licked and stroked his way across her smooth skin from the sweet dip of her waist to her belly button. She quivered under his ministrations, pleasing him with her responsiveness. Nikolai parted her legs and knelt between them. Placing his hands beneath her hips, he lifted her to his mouth.

"Don't make me wait too long. I've been thinking about sex with you for days. I'm so primed, I'll come if you breathe on my clit."

Nikolai parted her folds and took the time to study her pink labia and swollen bud. For some reason, the way she called what was between them sex rubbed him the wrong way. While he worried about the why, he trailed his fingers across her skin, damp with her arousal. Her hips jerked in his hold, and when he looked up, he saw she glared at him. He teased her feminine flesh with his fingers and savored her reaction. Open and honest with not a single pretense.

Unlike Laura.

He pushed the thought away to concentrate on Summer. He bent to rake his tongue along her cleft and clit. God, he couldn't get enough of the taste of her. She tensed at the touch, her eyes fluttered closed, and a throaty groan escaped her. Nikolai watched the changes in her body with fascination. He'd never paid much attention or cared after Laura, but watching her come, feeling the pulsating walls of her sex really did it for him.

"I thought I told you not to do that," she

said, sounding cross. "I want you inside me."

"Ah, but now I've taken off the edge, I get to make you hot all over again. Let me tell you what I'm going to do to you."

"What?" she whispered, sounding enthralled. "Tell me."

Nikolai let her hips fall to the bed. "First, I'm going to tie your hands to the bedhead so you can't distract me."

"Really?"

"Yeah. And because I know you'd cheat and open your eyes, you're going to lie facedown."

"You'll see my butt."

"Yeah."

"It's daylight."

"You didn't seem too worried before when you pranced into the house ahead of me."

"I was angry. I forgot. You know,

it's not my best feature." She cupped her breasts in her hands. "Wouldn't you rather feast your eyes on these beauties?"

He felt the corners of his eyes crinkle. "Next time. Turn over."

She resisted, a faint pucker between her brows. "Do you have to tie me up?"

Nikolai slid up the bed and pulled her into his arms. "We're not going to do anything you're unhappy with. Making love is about giving and receiving pleasure." He kissed her with an open-mouthed kiss, feasting on the curves of her lips and the minty moistness of her breath. When they parted, they were both breathing heavily. "It's about trust."

"I'm frightened you'll hurt me—"

"You like to stay in control." That made two of them. But she was so damn reckless at times, stubbornly trying to gain independence. Nikolai shook his head, knowing she was still in danger because of swapping that book. This marriage would be interesting. They might fight, but they'd have a hell of a time making up afterward.

"I don't like being told what to do. When I'm asked, that's different."

"So if I asked you to please turn over, would you do it?"

Her blue eyes were wide and dark with a trace of uncertainty as she studied him. Nikolai held his breath—waiting. She shifted, her belly rubbing the tip of his shaft. A pained gasp squeezed between his lips, and he prayed she made up her mind fast.

"I'll do it on the condition you let me tie you up in return."

"God, I've created a monster," he said

with a grin to soften the words. "We'll save the tying up for an hour or so. Where's this toy I've been hearing about?"

Summer's curious gaze passed over his condom-encased cock and turned distinctly hungry. Her brows rose and fell in a comical manner, but yep, that look was predatory.

"Maybe a little later for that too?"

"Good idea." Nikolai grasped her hips, positioned his cock at the mouth of her pussy and surged inside her tight, silken sheath with one hard thrust. Hot pleasure spilled through him as he pumped his cock with slow, deliberate strokes. He bent to feast on her mouth, their tongues twirling together in an imitation of their lovemaking. Nikolai broke off their kiss, his hands tugging her brown-and-blue hair from

the loose knot thing she'd contrived.
"That's better," he murmured, as damp
locks tumbled around her face. "Now
you look like a fallen woman."

A gurgle escaped her right before
she bit him on the biceps. Her sharp
teeth sent a signal straight to his dick.
He quickened his strokes, relishing the
leap of pleasure and the powerful
kick of sensation. It spilled through
him in a steady stream, like nothing
else he'd ever experienced before. Shit,
he hoped she was close because he
was going to come. He tried to slow
his impending release, but his senses
seemed heightened as he explored her
curvy body. He savored the scent on
her skin, the flowery smell of damp
hair, the slide of their sweat-slicked
bodies against each other, the salty taste
when he scraped his teeth across the

underside of her breast. He failed the quest for slow. F for failure. The taste of coconut exploded on his senses as he drew hard on her flesh. The gnawing ache in his dick intensified.

"Nikolai," she gasped.

Thank you! Nikolai chanted silently. Thank you. His hands dropped to cup her buttocks and he lifted her to deepen the angle of his strokes. Flesh slapped. Quicker. Harder. Summer dug her nails into his back. He felt the tightening clasp of her womb and molten fire erupted from his cock. A dark sound squeezed past his clenched teeth seconds before his seed poured from him in a long, never-ending stream. He kept thrusting, short, hard jabs, until the last ounce of pleasure was wrung from him.

Nikolai came to himself again when she started to squirm beneath him. "Am I squashing you?"

"S'okay." Summer gasped. "Too many curves anyway."

He chuckled and rolled so she lay on top of him. "Sweetheart, I like your curves just the way they are. A good, big handful."

"Yeah, anywhere you choose to grab," she said, her tone rueful.

"I like it." Nikolai smoothed one hand down her back and squeezed her rounded butt gently. "A lot."

"You're good for a woman's ego." She looked up at him, a renewed flare of desire in her blue eyes.

He drew a breath, deep and unsteady. "I hate to say it, but I don't think I can manage another go-around. Not yet. The mind is willing. The flesh needs to recuperate."

"No problem," Summer said in a breezy

voice that made the hairs at the back of his neck stand to cautious attention.

She climbed off him, their joined bodies separating. Once again, she bent over her bag to rummage through the contents, giving him a great view of her pussy and butt. He raked his gaze across her ample arse, his hands literally itching to touch. Shit, even better. He could sink his teeth in—he could bite. A surge of possessiveness flooded him without warning. Damn, he wanted to mark her fine-looking butt. He wanted his brand on her so no other man would make the mistake of thinking she was free.

A mischievous giggle drew his attention. She was busy watching him watch her.

"Minx. Come here." Nikolai yanked the spent condom off his cock and put it aside. He held his cock in his hand

and slowly pumped. His semi-erect dick reacted predictably to the stimulation.

"Ah-ha! There you are," she crooned, and she glanced at him with a blaze of sexual heat in her face. As he watched, the soft tones of arousal crawled down her neck to her chest. "My toy."

She yanked the wrapping off with all the enthusiasm of a child at Christmastime. Then she crawled across the bed to him on her hands and knees. Summer lay down across his chest, holding her toy up for him to see. "Feel how soft that is." Her hand caressed the red flexible skin, and Nikolai felt an answering surge in his cock as though she massaged him. "And look—it's got different speeds." A soft whine sounded. "But it doesn't grunt like you."

"You are in need of a good, hard spanking, Summer Williams."

"Okay," she said. "After we try the toy, and I tie you up."

Chapter 16

"Summer!" a masculine voice hollered. The angry sound echoed and bounced off the walls in a too-familiar manner.

"Oh, no," Summer muttered. Somehow, she didn't think closing her eyes and pretending she was asleep would solve this one.

Nikolai slithered from the bed and pulled an ugly-looking gun from under the bed.

"Don't go. Did you lock the bedroom door?"

"No."

"Summer!" The second voice sounded a shade deeper but just as angry.

"Shit, there's two of them," Nikolai said,

and he grabbed his jeans and yanked them on.

"Unfortunately."

Nikolai cast her a strange look, but the thump of heavy boots outside the bedroom forestalled his questions.

"Don't come in!" Summer shrieked. "I don't have any clothes—"

The door burst open and crashed against the bedroom wall. Two huge men paused at the threshold, and the four of them stared at each other with varying reactions.

"Fuck," Nikolai said in a fierce undertone.

Summer nodded.

Yep, this was a situation that called for a stronger word than "shit".

She tugged the covers up to her chin and considered crawling right underneath to hide. She thought about it for all of two seconds and cast away the cowardly idea. Someone needed to referee. She was the lone candidate.

"What the hell are you doing?" Dillon, her oldest brother, roared. He balanced lightly on his toes, his biceps bulging beneath his T-shirt. His dark hair stuck up, appearing as ruffled as his temper.

Josh, her other brother, folded his arms across his broad chest. He didn't smirk but the glint in his baby-blue eyes said he wanted to. "Oh, it's obvious what they've been doing," he drawled, confirming her supposition. The louse thought this was funny.

"Tarei." A pulse throbbed at Dillon's temple, and he looked as if he wanted to haul Nikolai from the room and beat him to a pulp. "Jake said Summer was here. Didn't expect you, too."

"Sex," Josh added helpfully.

Summer swallowed despite her best efforts to keep her anxiety contained. Her week just kept getting better. Murder, a little sex, and a fistfight chucked in for good measure. She had it all. Who needed to read the Sunday tabloids?

"I don't want to think about my sister and sex in the same sentence," Dillon snapped.

"Especially with him." Josh shifted his weight and clenched and unclenched his fists. The ever-present humor in his baby-looking face riled Summer. Time to take control.

"Out," she snapped, trying to ignore the fine tremor of nerves that shook her limbs.

"Fine." Dillon glared at Nikolai. "He can come with us."

"I don't think so," she returned sweetly.

If they laid one hand on Nikolai, so help her… She would Tae Kwon Do her two soldier brothers. "Nikolai stays with me."

Dillon and Josh exchanged glances.

Summer narrowed her eyes. "He stays with me. He's seen me dress before."

"I don't think they want to hear that, sweetheart."

"Fuck, no." Dillon jerked his head toward the door. "Out, Tarei. You're coming with us."

"You do know Nikolai?" Summer glanced from brother to brother. Their hard faces gave away little, but she guessed they weren't telling her something big. Fine. She'd worm the information from Nikolai the minute she got rid of her brothers.

Summer sat and made a show of grabbing the covers. The sheet slipped dangerously close to flashing her nipples.

"Aw, Summer!" Josh said, starting to back away. He grabbed his brother's arm and yanked.

Dillon resisted until Summer made another move. "The kitchen in five minutes," he ordered. "A second longer and we'll come back and drag you out."

Her brothers exited the room, their remarks to each other peppered with enough swear words it was a wonder her mother didn't make an appearance with her bar of soap.

Summer scrambled from the bed and searched for clothes. "I don't care what they said, I'm having a shower before I face them. And you are coming with me to explain what my brothers are talking about and why they don't like you. The bathroom has a lock."

Twenty minutes later, Summer sailed

into the kitchen with Nikolai trailing her.

"Coffee?" she asked Nikolai.

"Thanks."

"Don't think you can waltz in here and act like nothing has happened." Dillon paced the length of the kitchen like a big cat confined to a cage. "Mum's not going to be happy when she hears."

Fury made her jaw clench. "What? You gonna tell tales? It's about time you all realized I'm an adult. I'm not a sickly kid anymore. And I'll sleep with whomever I damn well want. If I want to sleep with an entire rugby team, then I will."

"Over my dead body," Nikolai snapped, curling a possessive arm around her waist and hauling her against his side.

"For that, we might let you live," Josh conceded.

"But you can keep your hands off our sister."

Nikolai didn't appear perturbed by her brother's posturing, so Summer allowed herself to relax a fraction. She was old enough to make her own decisions, and if some of them were wrong, they were her consequences to fix. By herself. She silently acknowledged her reckless streak, but she was working on that and trying to temper her reactions to new situations with thought first. Sometimes it worked.

Nikolai ignored her brothers and brushed a lock of hair from her face. He pressed a kiss to the spot of skin he'd uncovered and captured one of her hands to trace the fine skin at the inside of her wrist. "We're engaged. We're getting married."

Summer was so busy concentrating on the fiery sensation racing from her wrist and down her body, she didn't register his words at first.

"Married?" Josh glanced at Dillon.

Summer's mouth dropped open. Had he said married? She thought they'd discussed that earlier and come to an agreement. About to argue, she decided silence might be the wiser course. A glance at her brothers and their silent communication confirmed this course of action. She'd take issue with Nikolai and his high-handedness later.

"That's okay then." Dillon's grudging tone didn't fit his words. "We'd better ring Mum and let her know the news."

Okay, that did it. "I'm not marrying Nikolai."

Silence fell, broken by the roar of the next-door neighbor's lawnmower. Nikolai stiffened beside her, his hand gripping hers tightly. Dammit, enough. Time to pack a bag, call a cab and see if she could stay with Angel.

She wrenched her hand from Nikolai's and stomped to the door. She flinched inwardly at the burst of angry heat caused by three soldiers glaring at her back.

Too bad.

They could settle their fight by themselves, and if they wanted to pound each other into the ground let them.

"Summer!" Nikolai roared.

"I'm fed up with you all shouting orders at me. I won't marry you. You haven't asked me." Was it too much to ask for a little romance? When had proposing on bended knee gone out of fashion? Dammit, she wanted roses and sweet talk.

Summer kept walking and threw open the bedroom door. The rumpled bed reminded her of how good it felt when

Nikolai was holding her, his cock tightly wedged in her pussy. Too bad memories would have to sustain her because she wasn't putting up with commands. They might belong to the army, but she didn't, and it was about time they remembered this fact.

Boots thundered on the wooden floor behind her. Great. The entire herd had come to watch her pack. Fine.

"Care to offer suggestions as to the best place to pack these, boys?" Summer held up the box of glow-in-the-dark condoms, with the label facing outward and clearly visible. Mrs. Ferguson would have been proud. She'd listened carefully during their marketing seminar.

Josh sniggered. "I wouldn't wear those if you paid me."

"He better have worn them," Dillon

growled.

Nikolai tensed noticeably and shot an irritable look at Summer. "I didn't, which is why we're getting married."

"Bastard."

Dillon and Josh rounded on Nikolai. A fist flew. She wasn't sure which brother the punch came from, but it connected with Nikolai's jaw. Before she knew it, fists were going in all directions along with realistic crunches and spurts of blood.

"Stop it!" She threw the box of condoms at Dillon's head. Green foil packets rained down, landing all over the floor. Something else to throw. She grabbed the nearest thing to hand. The fly-fishing book. She heaved it at Josh. Bull's eye! The book hit the back of his head, bounced off and thumped to the floor while she searched for another missile.

At a loss, she glanced back in time to see Nikolai clip Dillon's jaw with a well-directed punch. Dillon's head snapped back. He dodged to avoid a second punch, and his foot landed on the book. It skidded from under him, but Dillon balanced like the panther he resembled and kicked the fly-fishing book aside. It crashed against the wall.

The book.

Something to heave at her brothers again. When she scooped it up, a tightly wadded piece of paper fell from the damaged spine. Sudden excitement pounded through her. A reason Dare wanted the book. "Nikolai!" she shrieked.

The three men ignored her cry. Nikolai took a blow in the stomach, roared, and came up swinging his fists. Dillon ducked, stepped back and bumped Josh. Josh dodged but collided with her. She squeaked in alarm as they fell to the floor in a tangle of limbs and a loud thump.

"Get off me, you great big oaf!" She pushed at her brother, but he was slow to move and felt like a giant sack of potatoes draped across her chest. "Can't breathe."

"Get off her, dammit." Nikolai came to the rescue.

Seconds later, the weight lifted from her chest, and Josh thumped onto the mat beside the bed.

"You okay, sweetheart?" He helped her sit up and brushed her hair from her eyes. "Do you need your inhaler?"

"Inhaler? God, Summer. You haven't used your inhaler for over a year," Dillon said.

"No, I'm fine. Josh knocked the wind out of me. Is he okay?" She peered past

Dillon's worried face to study Josh who was rubbing the side of his head in a groggy manner.

"Nah, he's got a hard head. He'll be fine," Dillon said. "I'm more worried about you. I thought you'd grown out of the asthma attacks."

"Dillon, for the last time, I'm fine. If or when I'm not feeling well, I'll take myself off to the doctor. I don't need my family treating me like a baby. Nikolai, look what fell out of the book when the spine broke. I didn't think of breaking the binding."

"We've got more important things to worry about than a damn book," Dillon said.

"Summer is in—"

Summer placed a hand on Nikolai's shoulder and squeezed hard. "I'll tell them since it was my fault. I've got myself in a spot of trouble—"

"Why didn't you call us instead of him?" Josh climbed to his feet and rubbed his head. "We're family."

"She came to me," Nikolai snapped.

Summer drew in a sharp breath, and warmth tugged at her heartstrings. Maybe there was hope for this particular soldier, if he thought of them as a unit. She pulled a face. No, not a unit. That smacked of army and military. Team? No. Perhaps couple. Shying from the idea, even though it made her warm and tingly inside, she unfolded the tightly wadded up paper.

Marina, berth C49, Seraphina.

Summer frowned. That was it?

"What trouble?" Dillon demanded.

"This is an address for a marina. Weird. Why hide it in a book? Why not email or phone?"

"Summer, what trouble?" Dillon thundered.

She bit her lip. "I met a man and—"

Dillon sliced a black glower in Nikolai's direction. "Him?"

"Will you let me finish? Five minutes tops. Then you can do your shouting. More impact that way."

"Mum was too lenient with you," Josh said. "Should have paddled your backside."

"Nope," she said. "The only one who gets to do that is Nikolai. Do you want me to tell you or not?"

"Continue," Nikolai said, a dangerous glint in his eyes. "About the clotheshorse. Not the other. We'll discuss that later."

Summer brightened. "Tonight?"

"Enough," Dillon snapped.

Summer bit back the building grin.

Her big brother looked distinctly uncomfortable, but he was playing dumb. She made a mental note to use the ploy as a distraction again.

"Yeah," Josh sniggered. "I'm thinking this discussion doesn't have much to do with punishment."

"I met Dare Martin, and we went out together a few times. When I started getting serious about Nikolai, I tried to break it off with Dare. It was strange," she mused. "He's not stupid but he acted thick as a plank of wood when I tried to end things. He asked me out for dinner."

"You didn't tell me that," Nikolai said.

"He knew I used to visit the same bookshop he patronized, and when he asked me to pick up a package of books for him now and then, I didn't think anything of it. But one night, I opened his package of books. The title was a duplicate of the first one I received by mistake. That's how we met," she added. "I thought it was strange, so I found another copy and exchanged them. Then the owner of the bookshop was found murdered. The police are calling it a robbery gone wrong. I think it had something to do with me exchanging books. Dare wanted this message."

Josh groaned long and theatrically. "Jeez, Summer. Why didn't you just go and stick your hand into the lion's mouth?"

Irritation bloomed without warning. "Shut up, or I'll give you a matching lump on the other side of your thick head. I agree it wasn't the wisest course of action, but it's too late now. I need help, not 'I told you so'."

"Why didn't you control her?" Dillon growled at Nikolai.

"Excuse me?" Nikolai straightened. "We are talking about Summer."

Dillon glanced at his sister and shrugged. "Point taken. So, what do we do now?"

"I've already spoken to the police," Nikolai said, tugging the paper from her hand. "Jake's brother is a cop. I'll take the book and the paper to him. My guess is that his communication is being monitored and this is a way to get information under the radar."

Dillon nodded.

Josh grunted his approval.

"What are we talking about? Drugs?" Summer scowled. As usual, they were treating her like a child, patting her on the head and expecting her to go along with their plans. Her mouth tightened to a mutinous line. "I'll go to the police with you. They'll want to talk to me."

Nikolai frowned at her. "No, it's too dangerous."

Dillon and Josh repeated their nods and grunts of endorsement.

Summer huffed and went back to her packing. Ignoring the bossy men, she picked up the green foil packets and tossed them into her overnight bag. She crammed in her clothes and stomped down the hall to the bathroom to collect her toiletries.

Somehow, without saying a word, Dillon and Josh had gotten to Nikolai, and he was backing off. She wanted to curse. She wanted to screech. Instead, she did nothing and concentrated on packing.

"Good," Dillon said. "I'm glad you're packing. You can come with us."

Summer stilled. "Where?"

"We'll go to Uncle Henry's tonight

and back to Eketahuna tomorrow. You should be safe there."

"What about my job? If I leave, I won't get my certificate."

"You can do it another time," Dillon said.

Summer sucked in a deep breath, ready to hurl a curse or two. Her job was important. She might not make world-altering decisions or save lives like them, but she made people happy. She glanced at Nikolai, half expecting him to protest, but the stupid man didn't utter a word. Fine. Now she knew where she stood in his list of priorities.

Prison must feel like this.

Her two brothers hovered over her while she watered Uncle Henry's rose garden. They tensed at the purr and rumble of each car and made a nuisance of themselves until she wanted to scream. Frustration simmered as she turned off the water and rolled up the hose on Uncle Henry's special stand.

"I don't think you should see Nikolai again," Dillon said without warning.

Even though she'd expected this, her brother's words still riled her, stoking her slow-burning anger. "It's none of your business. I wouldn't think of telling you not to go out with Suzie Daniels when you're at home on leave, even though she's a gossip and jumps into bed with Tom McPherson the minute you leave town. Nope, wouldn't even consider telling you that." She turned her back on her oldest brother and came face-to-face with Josh's smirk.

"Help me out here," Dillon snapped. "You tell her. She won't listen to me."

The humor dropped from Josh, leaving an image of what he must look like in soldier mode. "Dillon's right. There are things you don't know about Tarei. Go home and date one of the boys there. I'm sure you're not lacking for offers."

"You're treating me like a defenseless child. None of you will tell me what happened with the police and the note. I'm tired of it. I am an adult. You can't stop me dating Nikolai." Rant done, she stormed inside, sensing rather than hearing her brothers follow. They weren't the only ones in trouble. Nikolai wasn't talking either.

"His wife and kid died," Dillon said in a hard voice. "After that, he wasn't the same. That's what I heard. On his last mission, one of his men got hit. Tarei left him to die."

Summer yanked open the fridge and

pulled out a bottle of wine.

"I'll do it," Josh said, coming up behind her and trying to take possession of the wine.

"The top is a screw-cap. I can open it without your help. I'm sick of you all trying to run my life." Tears stung her eyes, and her voice took on a choked, thick quality. Her brothers exchanged a look of masculine panic. Give them a man with a gun and they knew what to do, but a woman in tears put a spoke in their he-man bravado. What did she have to do to convince them she didn't need looking after?

The phone rang, and Dillon went to answer.

"I'll get it. I can manage that without interference." She grabbed the phone on the eighth ring, after her brother stepped away, hands raised in surrender. "Yes?" she said, her narrowed eyes still on her brothers. As soon as she got the chance, she intended to confront Nikolai. "Hello?" she repeated impatiently.

"Girly, we know you have the book," a gruff voice said.

She put the phone on speaker. "What book? Is this the bookshop where I special ordered? The Pen and Quill?"

"Don't play dumb, girly. We want that book."

Her brothers closed in on her, one standing either side in silent protection. In this instant, it felt good to have them on her team, offering moral support. Ironic. "Who is this?" A healthy dose of fear rose, and she struggled to keep her voice even. They'd already killed once to get their hands on the book.

"Do you recognize the voice?" Josh

whispered.

Summer shook her head.

"Put the book in the mailbox, and it will be collected with no questions asked."

"But I don't have—"

"Do it or else." The phone slammed down, the anger behind the crash raising a rash of gooseflesh on her arms and legs.

"He wants the book." Summer stared at her brothers. "What do I do?"

Dillon and Josh exchanged a look before stepping away to huddle.

"Still trying to exclude me? Fine." She stomped from the kitchen and slammed into her bedroom. The room shuddered at the force of her anger. A small bottle of perfume, balancing precariously on the edge of her dresser, toppled to the floor. Of course, she hadn't put the lid on properly and it parted company from the bottle. The perfume gushed onto the carpet before she could grab it. The perfume's floral notes tickled her nose and a sneeze erupted. Probably time to tidy her messy room.

She sorted dirty laundry into a pile and consigned clean clothes to drawers and the wardrobe. Instantly, the room looked better. She peered out the window at Nikolai's house. Before she'd even formulated the thought, she was sliding the window up. At least this time her jeans offered better protection against Uncle Henry's rose bushes.

She slithered over the windowsill and dropped into the garden below. In the hour before darkness, the scent of roses filled the air along with the moist, damp soil. She felt another sneeze building, and knew she needed to move fast before her brothers came to investigate.

Her shirt caught and a part of a rose bush shot underneath to tear the tender skin at the small of her back. Wincing, she extricated herself then frantically grabbed her nose. Too late. The sneeze escaped. A feeble one, but a noise, nonetheless. She froze, waiting for a stampede of brothers. When nothing happened, she sighed in relief and crept across the open section of lawn before cautiously opening the gate and letting herself into Nikolai's property.

The faint sound of an approaching car hurried her along. Summer hustled across the deck, dodging the broken board as she headed for Nikolai's bedroom window.

A smile flickered across her face when she saw it was open, the net curtain dancing in the soft breeze. She slipped inside.

Chapter 17

Someone tackled her. Nikolai, she thought with relief as she identified his soap and distinctive masculine scent. His hand curled around her breast before she could speak.

"Why, Mr. Tarei, I do believe you have a boob fetish."

"Only for yours," he whispered, his hand shaping and testing the weight of her breast. He nuzzled the soft skin at the base of her neck and scraped his teeth across, taking a tiny nip. "God, I missed you." He tugged the cotton fabric of her shirt to expose more skin and pressed a kiss to her collarbone before reaching to flick on a lamp.

She gave a breathless laugh, surprised by his admission.

"If you're pregnant we're getting married," he said in a tight voice.

It was as if he made the offer under duress and his words and tone stung. "I never asked you to marry me. I don't want marriage." Not if I'm ordered.

Was it too much to expect a declaration of love? They were good together, if only he'd quit worrying about the age difference and his past.

"You're right not to want marriage with me."

His hollow defeat made her want to protest. "Are we talking about your wife? Or the man Dillon says you left?"

Nikolai froze, his expression going hard. "You believe him?"

"No, I don't. I know you. You would do everything you could to save a friend."

A strand of tension released in her when she uttered the confident words because she believed them with every particle of her being. Nikolai was a hero.

"Thanks." The tautness left him, his warrior's face relaxing. "My wife—"

"Sounds to me as if she was selfish, thinking of herself and her needs, instead of considering you as well."

He met her gaze with honesty. "She was young, and I was away a lot of the time. It was hard for her."

"Stop right there." She placed her palm on his sternum. "Don't draw parallels. I have a job, friends, interests. I am not selfish and self-absorbed like your wife."

"No, but you're reckless. You leap without thinking. Do your brothers know you've left the house?"

"No," she whispered, guilt surfacing to replace her former anger. His accusation stung. "I'd better ring them. But I'm not going back. I want to stay with you and...talk."

A chuckle rumbled against her hand. "Is talk a euphemism for sex?"

"Could be if you play your cards right. Can I use your phone?"

Something that could have been approval glinted in his brown eyes as he tossed her his phone. Suddenly breathless, her hand shook when she dialed Uncle Henry's number.

"Dillon, it's me." Summer held the phone away from her ear and waited for her brother to stop shouting. When silence ensued, she put the phone back next to her ear.

"I am next door with Nikolai. No. You don't need to come and get me. I'm perfectly safe. And to be doubly sure, we'll use condoms." She paused. "I love you too, Dillon," she said sweetly. "Seriously though, we have Nikolai's cell phone. If we have any problems, we will call you."

"Sounded as if that went well." He leaned against his pillows, his gaze skimming her face and settling on her lips.

"Oh, yeah. I've noticed a mention of sex diverts the yelling."

"What about if I were to mention sex?"

"I'd say 'excellent idea'." She stroked his cheek, tested the dark stubble on his jaw and dallied to trace his lips with her finger. Nikolai opened his mouth and took her finger inside, closing his lips and surrounding her with warmth. A tingle sprang to life in her breasts. She imagined his mouth drawing on her nipples instead of her finger and the tingle intensified to a pulse. Juices moistened her lace panties, making her squirm. "And I'd say when will we get to the action—"

Nikolai tugged the fabric clinging to her hips. "You're the one wearing clothes."

Summer bent up to brush a teasing kiss on his mouth and climbed off the bed. Her heart zinged at his teasing. She really liked him in this mood. "You provide the music, and I'll strip."

Nikolai flicked on a radio. In dulcet tones, the female announcer read out the news. "Music," he said, his brows rising in a silent dare.

Summer smiled, blew him a kiss, and wriggled her hips in a suggestive bump. His eyes rounded slightly but zeroed in on her swaying hips and breasts. Huh! Didn't take much to snare a male's attention. She waggled her boobs, the heavy globes swaying beneath her cotton shirt. Then she reached under the fabric and flicked her bra open, spilling her breasts free from the lacy bit of nothing. Deft fingers separated button from buttonhole until her shirt gaped, giving Nikolai peek-a-boo glances of the curves of her breasts and the occasional flash of nipple.

His intent gaze warmed her until her body hummed. She ambled a little closer, and a rumble of approval sounded. A slow grin bloomed on his face, stoking her wavering courage. This stripper routine was harder than it seemed. Her hands fluttered to the dome snap on her jeans. With a brief prayer for gracefulness, she wriggled from the denim, only to hit a snag.

"Forgotten something, sweetheart?" Laughter echoed in his voice, bringing a wave of flustered color to her cheeks.

Hot damn. Her shoes. Back to stripper school for her. She struggled like an ungainly stork while she dealt with the laces on her shoes. Finally free, she sucked in a deep breath and rolled her shoulders to flash her breasts. Yep, that got his attention. She strutted the length of the room, prancing like a show pony.

"Is that it?" A devilish grin twisted his lips. "All I've seen is a flash of tits. Can't see much else because of that baggy thing you're wearing." He made a tsk-tsking sound and shook his head in mock disappointment.

At least she hoped it was mockery. It would be terrible to send him to sleep when she was starting to get off on this stripping number. "I obviously need training. Perhaps I could get a job in a topless bar. There were ads in the Herald the other day."

Nikolai sat up so quickly a pillow flew to the floor. Brown eyes narrowed while his smile vanished. "I don't think so. I'm not having my wife pedaling flesh in a bar."

His wife. Presumptuous of him. He needed to control that character flaw, especially if he expected her to fight her reckless nature. Summer peeled back her shirt, baring her boobs. She peeked at Nikolai to gauge the effect. Mission accomplished. Definite interest and distraction from the marriage topic.

She was not marrying him, and that was final.

Suddenly tired of games, she flung off her shirt and let it drop onto the carpet. She pushed her panties down her legs and kicked them aside to strike a pose. "Interested?"

His eyes darkened with sensual heat. "Come here."

She strolled to the bed, making sure she put an extra wiggle in her walk. Her breasts swayed, the sparks of desire igniting within her. No longer unhurried, she launched herself at him, trusting him to catch her.

He did. His arms tightened around her as their naked bodies aligned. He kissed her fiercely. Hungrily. Forcing her to concentrate on him, and leaving no room for distracting thoughts of marriage, crooks or family. The kiss softened, and his tongue explored. She shuddered and undulated against him, savoring the bulk of masculine muscles and the fierce jut of his cock against her belly. Juices seeped from her, her body softening, almost pleading for his hard cock.

Nikolai pulled away from her, breathing

hard. He brushed the messy strands of hair from her face, sexual hunger roaring through him. "You're addictive. You know that? I can't stop thinking about you. About being with you. Being in you."

Nikolai slid a hand down her bare back and reveled in the satin-smooth texture of her skin. It was true. Each minute spent with her anchored him tighter. Like a silken trap, but he'd stopped fighting for freedom. Each time he mentioned marriage, the word slipped easier off his tongue.

Marriage to Summer Williams would be different from his time with Laura. Summer would fight for her independence. She'd expect it. When he left with his unit, she wouldn't pine away. She'd get on with her life. Yet knowing that didn't worry him. Despite her youth, she bore integrity.

He trusted her.

Nikolai breathed deeply, drawing a lungful of Summer essence and flowers. He'd always thought of flowers as girly. Now he thought of her. He cupped her bottom and slid one thigh between hers. He drew flush with her feminine flesh, the heat he encountered sending a jerk of impatience the length of his cock.

"You want me," he whispered, part of him in awe. All they'd done was kiss, yet she was ready for him. The knowledge made him feel god-like.

"Always," she said, running her fingers across his chest. The light scratching and pinching of her fingers sent a jolt of lust soaring. She massaged his chest with one hand, digging in and retracting her nails like a cat, and damn if he didn't want to purr.

Nikolai leaned over to jerk the bedside drawer open. He grabbed a condom packet, ripped it open and rolled it on his dick. With one hard thrust, he slid into her tight channel. Summer clenched her inner muscles, making her flesh tighten around his girth. A repeat move forced a groan past his clenched lips. Helpless under her spell, he withdrew and thrust, increasing his pace when she moved with him, clutching his shoulders, still digging her fingernails into his skin.

Another drive sent sensation rippling from his cock. He quickened his strokes, savoring the slap of flesh against flesh, the pain of Summer's fingernails and the small whimpers she made at the back of her throat.

He gripped her hips and pounded into her. He was close to climax. He wanted to keep thrusting hard and fast until his seed spewed from him, but he wanted her pleasure too. Desperately needed this. His hand slipped between them to dance across her swollen clit. He massaged lightly and gritted his teeth, trying to hold back.

"Nikolai." She cried out in pleasure. "Nikolai."

"Come for me, sweetheart." His finger slid back and forth, 'round and 'round, and he couldn't prevent another plunge into her hot depths. One more plunge was all it took for him to explode. Spasm after spasm shook his body. Then Summer tumbled into climax, gripping his cock in her silken flesh. He swallowed his groan at the vise of pleasure that gripped mind and body. Fuck, he was in trouble here and wise enough to know it.

Nikolai woke alert and ready to fight. Training had taught him to assimilate the situation without moving a muscle. He listened intently, trying to work out what had woken him. The moon shone through the window, aiding his vision. Summer slept on, her mouth slightly open. Her chest rose and fell and a faint whistle sounded, followed by a snort.

His lips quirked. Something to tease her about.

A floorboard squeaked, wiping his amusement clean. Someone was inside the house. He untangled his limbs from her warm embrace and grabbed his jeans. His habit of leaving them on the floor right by the bed was good planning.

"Nikolai?" She stretched with no pretense at modesty, her mouth split wide in a yawn.

"Someone's inside the house."

She sprang from the bed and grabbed her clothes. "Dare?"

"Doubt it. He'd get someone else to do his dirty work."

Another board creaked at the far end of the passage.

"Ring your brothers." Nikolai didn't wait for her to answer but opened the bedroom door and slipped out.

She strained to hear anything out of place. Nothing. She shoved her arms into her shirt, getting tangled in her haste. "Breathe," she muttered, giving herself an old, familiar lecture.

A crash reverberated from the far end of the house. A muffled thud. Anxiety for Nikolai hastened her speed. Dressed, Summer grabbed the phone.

The bedroom door flew open before

she finished dialing.

"Put the phone down, girlie."

The man wasn't tall—about the same height as her—but his shoulders were bulky. When he switched on the light, she blinked. Her first clear look at his narrow, scarred face wasn't reassuring. Mean and determined. Fear jumped squarely in the middle of her stomach. She backed up toward the window. She'd come in that way—maybe she could leave via the same route.

She kept dialing, trying to concentrate despite the trembling fingers and her split attention. Sparring in the gym was different from confronting a man intent on injury.

"Put the fuckin' phone down." He had a smoker's voice, and it reacted on her like fingernails on a blackboard.

The crashes in the passage outside

increased in intensity. Didn't take a rocket scientist to know Nikolai was in trouble.

The man snarled, a sound from deep in his belly. "Girlie, don't make me tell you a third time." He kept coming and closed the distance between them with a flying leap. Summer danced out of the way, trying to breathe through her panic. The rasp of her lungs indicated a need to calm herself, before she went into a full-blown asthma attack. If she did that, she'd be about as useful as a book with missing pages.

The wooden screech of a rising window sounded behind her. She whirled in time to see another man climbing through the window into the room. The smug expression on his freckled face fueled anger. Fine. She was cornered. She admitted it, but that didn't mean all was lost. She placed the phone down on the dressing table and stepped away.

The door opened without warning, and someone thrust Nikolai inside. A trickle of blood ran down one cheek, and his hands were tied behind his back. She bit back a cry, knowing she needed to keep calm.

Breathe, she reminded herself.

Nikolai's calm demeanor helped her focus. Their gazes met in silent communication. His was hot with fury. Pissed and in warrior mode.

Summer suppressed a swallow and looked away. Two men followed—one a stranger and the other very familiar.

Summer's chin jerked upward. "What are you doing here, Dare?"

"I want the book, Summer. I know you have it."

"The book I picked up for you? I gave it

to the hostess at your restaurant. Didn't she give it to you?"

"Quit with the cute stuff. I know you have it—process of elimination. Give me the book and no one will get hurt."

She didn't believe him for a minute. Beneath the city gloss lurked a shark. She saw it now—clearly, just as Nikolai had warned. Dare had killed already or one of his men had without giving a second thought to the victim or his family. She hoped the hostess at his restaurant was alive to tell the tale.

"The book." Dare stepped up to her and slapped her across the face.

Summer stumbled back with the force of the blow.

Nikolai growled and flung himself at Dare. He didn't get far. The freckled man kicked him in the stomach, and he fell to the ground.

She raised a hand to her hot cheek and glared at Dare. "I don't have your book."

"Come, love. You can do better than that."

"Boss, I'll make her talk," the freckled man said.

Summer darted him a look and inwardly shuddered. The way he scanned her up and down sent loathing crawling across her skin. A combination of mean and stupid blazed from his open face. She didn't want to go near the man.

"I'd love to feel those tits of hers. Bet they're real. Not those false jobbies."

"Maybe later, Ross." Dare smirked at Summer, obviously sensing her unease and happy to foster her fear. "Give me the book, and I'll let you go."

"She said she doesn't know what you're talking about," Nikolai said.

"I didn't ask you. Get him on his feet. We'll take him to the warehouse. If he gives you any trouble, knock him out."

Summer's stomach lurched, the nagging knowledge that this situation was her fault making her feel ill. What should she do? Did she tell the truth? That the police had the book, or did she try to stall? Neither option looked good. Bottom line—the book wasn't hers to give.

But perhaps...

"The book is in my room next door." And so were her brothers. She turned in that direction and whirled back on hearing a thump. She bit back a cry of horror. They'd hit Nikolai on the back of the head.

"Nice try, my dear. It's not. The house was searched last night, so we don't need to waste time searching again or bother about coming face-to-face with the two men currently in residence."

Summer wrinkled her nose and aimed for ditzy. "If you've misplaced your book, why don't you buy another?"

"Like you did." Dare studied her with a dispassionate look, unfazed by her act. "This is what we're going to do. Take the boyfriend to the warehouse. We'll release him once you return the book."

"What about me, boss?" the freckled one said. "What should I do?"

"Go with the others. One drive and the other two sit in the back with him." Dare jerked his head in Nikolai's direction. "If he regains consciousness, make sure he doesn't get away."

"What about her?"

Summer held her breath. If Dare intended to send the others with Nikolai, she might have a chance to get free. A slim chance—if she kept her wits about her.

"Summer and I are going to have a little chat." Dare's face hardened, giving her an inkling of his determination. In that instant, fear dug in its claws. He was determined to reclaim his book. Nikolai and her brothers were right. She was in over her head.

Chapter 18

"Just showing you how serious I am, my dear."

Summer scowled and bit her lip to keep the horrified tears at bay. Dare's three men had hauled Nikolai from his bedroom unconscious and bleeding, and there hadn't been a thing she could do to stop the beating. "I am not 'your dear'."

"No," Dare said, prowling around her and looking her up and down like a piece of merchandise. "You're his whore."

The air whistled through her teeth as she sucked in an affronted breath. Who the hell was he to call her a whore when he was into crime and murder? Outside a car started and pulled away. Gradually the sound faded, leaving her alone with Dare.

She'd wanted independence, and now she had it big-time, she wanted the comfort of her bossy, nosy family.

And Nikolai.

"What? Nothing to say for yourself? You would have made a good wife for me Summer. Young. Intelligent. My parents liked you. You would've made a good mother for my children. Even bloody Ngataki saw my interest."

"Who?"

"Never mind."

He sauntered around the bed, assured and confident in his ability to handle her. Summer waited until he was within range, her heart hammering with a combination of bloodlust and anticipation. Cocky little twerp. Nikolai was worth ten of Dare Martin.

"I wouldn't take you now if you paid me," he drawled.

She sprang at him, lashing out with a kick to the head, her aggression taking him by surprise. His head snapped back, and she gloried in the shock that rippled across his face. Grunting, she kicked out again and stomped on his glossy, black leather shoes. He shouldn't underestimate a woman. A balled-up fist to the stomach made him hunch forward.

"Bitch," Dare spat, wary now as he stepped out of range.

"And proud of it," she snarled. "At least I'm not a coward."

Dare lunged at her, but she danced out of his way unscathed. She circled, watching his eyes, and feigned a punch to his upper chest in a move that would have made her teacher proud. When he reacted, she went low, sending a striking blow at Dare's groin. The animal scream of pain as he crumpled brought satisfaction. Bastard.

She rubbed her hands together in a job-well-done gesture. He deserved worse. Much worse, and by the time she was finished with him, he'd be sorry. She grabbed a belt and a black tie from the wardrobe and used them to bind Dare's arms and legs. Thanks to her brothers, she knew how to tie a decent knot.

Keeping a wary eye on Dare, she hurried for the cell phone.

"Yeah?"

Her brother sounded alert as if he'd been awake for hours. Must be a SAS thing. "It's me. Nikolai's in trouble. They took him away to a warehouse somewhere."

"Stay there," Dillon ordered.

The phone slammed down, and she nibbled her bottom lip before coming to a decision. She checked the numbers Nikolai had stored in his mobile and rang Jake.

He answered on the first ring, just as alert as her brother. "Yeah."

"It's Summer. Nikolai's in trouble."

"The book?"

"Yeah."

"Where are you?"

"At Nikolai's place."

"Louie and I'll be there soon. Don't do anything without us."

"Summer!" Her brother's holler echoed in the passageway. "Where the hell are you?"

"Down here."

Dare groaned, and she debated kicking him again.

"The bedroom," Dillon said. "I should have known."

"Who's he?" Josh said. "Doesn't look too healthy."

"That's Dare Martin. I kicked him in the testicles," she said with distinct relish. "Nikolai's friends, Jake and Louie, are coming to help. I don't know where they've taken Nikolai or what they're going to do with him. He was unconscious. This is my fault."

"Guess we can use their help," Dillon conceded.

"No blame game, Summer. Hold it together for Nikolai. He's tough," Josh said.

Summer turned to Dillon for added encouragement and found her brother glaring at the rumpled bed.

"Until I get my hands on him," Dillon snapped. He bent to check Dare. "Good job, sis. Doesn't look like he'll be going anywhere."

"But we need to find out where they've taken Nikolai," she said. "Dare can talk, right?"

"Go and wait for Jake and Louie. We'll talk to the clotheshorse."

"That's what Nikolai calls him," Summer said.

"We agree on something," Dillon said deadpan.

She rolled her eyes and walked from the bedroom without glancing back.

Daylight, early next morning

"What if we can't find Nikolai?" Summer demanded for about the fourth time. Disquieting thoughts, fueled by her vivid imagination, increased her uneasiness as she glanced from Dillon to Josh, who sat beside her in the rear of Louie's car. What if they'd hurt him even more? What if they'd killed him?

She'd been so busy fighting for independence and playing games she hadn't admitted to her feelings. She attempted to swallow the huge lump of fear working its way up her throat. What if it was too late?

"Can we gag her?" Josh asked.

Jake turned and grinned from the front passenger seat. "She's your sister. You gag her."

"Aren't you worried about Nikolai? He was unconscious. They killed the owner of the bookshop. And we've got no idea where he is." Her sentence ended on a pained whisper. She sensed the men glancing at each other in alarm. "I'm not crying," she gritted out.

Jake's cell phone rang. "Yeah? The intel

is good?"

Summer studied Jake as he listened, tension crawling through her stomach until she thought she might vomit. The tense set left his shoulders, and she let her breath ease out in relief. They knew—or had a good idea—of Nikolai's location.

"We'll meet you there," Jake said, confirming her guess. "East Tamaki. Cryers Road," he instructed Louie.

The car accelerated down the motorway.

Summer's hands twisted in her lap. Please let him be all right. She thought about his marriage proposal. Again. Ever since they'd dragged Nikolai from the bedroom, she'd worried about not telling him of her feelings. Stupid and stubborn to the finish—that was her. And don't forget reckless, her conscience prodded.

"Why don't you kick a girl when she's down?" she muttered.

"Huh?" Josh said.

On her other side, Dillon's gaze pushed holes in the side of her face.

Summer turned to glare at him. "What?"

"Our sister is losing it," Josh said.

Her gaze jerked back to Josh. "Your sister is in love with Nikolai Tarei," she snapped. "He's in danger because of me, and I'm worried sick."

"Go, Nik," Jake said from the front seat.

"What if something happens to him? It will be my fault."

Josh groaned, long and loud. "Will you shut up?"

"But—"

"In the glove box," Louie said.

Jake didn't ask questions but bent to

open the glove box as directed. He pulled out a navy-blue silk scarf and turned round to the back seat with a grin. "A silencer," he said.

Dillon snorted. Josh chuckled, but Summer stared, momentarily diverted from her worries. She'd glimpsed a second blue scarf in the glove box before Jake slammed it shut. "Do you tie up woman with those scarves?" she blurted.

For an instant, there was stunned silence, and all she could hear was the smooth purr of the car and the distant din of a siren.

"What kind of fool question is that?" Dillon demanded.

"Well, I don't know about you," Jake drawled, "but I'm kinda interested in the answer."

Josh stirred beside her. "Yeah."

"We're almost there," Louie said.

Jake groaned. "Aw, come on, mate. You can't leave us hanging like that."

"Don't answer," Dillon ordered. "Not with my baby sister in the car."

"She's not so little if she's doing the horizontal tango with Nik," Jake pointed out.

Both Josh and Dillon growled.

"That's enough," Summer said, placing a hand on each of them. "Louie, I'll discuss scarves with you later. Do you have any books on the subject?"

Jake threw back his head and roared with laughter. "Man, I'm not sure whether to feel sorry for Nikolai or envy him."

"You are not hooking up with Tarei," Dillon snarled.

Silence, tense and brittle, fell again. Summer's stomach hollowed out at the sudden chill inside the car.

Finally, Louie broke the silence. "Nik is our mate." The threat was implicit in his words. Do or say anything against Nikolai and suffer the consequences.

"He got a man killed. A good man," Dillon snarled. "Summer is staying away from him."

"I'm—"

"That's bullshit," Jake said in a quiet voice that made Summer shiver. He never came across as dangerous because he was always joking around. "You don't know what happened that day."

And don't judge. No matter what Dillon and Josh said about Nikolai, she wouldn't believe them. She knew him. He was gentle, caring and loyal. And she loved him.

"I know enough," Dillon said.

"A mate died that day because Tarei left

him," Josh snarled.

Jake scowled, and in that moment he looked like the dangerous hunter he was. "You weren't there. Everything you know is secondhand."

Summer suppressed a shiver at unleashed violence in his words.

"Tell us then, because we sure as hell aren't letting our sister within calling range of him. He left his man to die. Teammates don't do that."

Summer straightened. "You can't send me home to Eketahuna. I won't go."

When Nikolai was safe, they were going to talk. Then once she'd sorted things to her satisfaction, they would marry. But first, she was going to tell him how much she loved him.

In the front seat, Summer noticed Louie and Jake glancing at each other. After a few seconds, Louie spoke.

"Nik had the choice of saving a woman and her three kids or his man. He tried to do both and damn near killed himself. His leg is never gonna come right. Not one hundred percent."

"Do you have proof of this," Dillon demanded.

"Uncle Henry knows," Summer said with instinctive certainty. "But it doesn't matter. I trust Nikolai."

Louie glanced in the rear-vision mirror. "A Williams with commonsense. Thank you, God."

"Nikolai would give his left nut to save another life." Jake turned to fix her brothers with a steely glare. "Only old women listen to gossip. If you want the truth, ask Nikolai instead of condemning him without trial."

Summer laughed at Jake's fervent words while she felt her brothers wince at mention of the male anatomy.

"Good. We're all on the same page. Nikolai and I are a couple."

"With an interesting sex life," Jake added.

"I find it interesting," she conceded. "I learn something new every time."

"Summer, button it," Dillon snapped.

"Boys, we're here," Louie interrupted.

The men snapped into predator mode, and the tension ratcheted sharply upward inside the car.

"What if this isn't the right warehouse?" Summer asked.

Josh patted one jeans-clad knee, squeezing in gentle encouragement. "If it's not the right one, we'll keep trying."

"It's the right one," Jake said. "Dan sounded confident."

Louie slowed the car and drove past, then pulled up at the end of the street.

"Anyone see life?"

A croak of protest leaked from Summer's tight throat.

"Sorry. Poor word choice," Louie said.

They climbed from the car, shutting the doors with careful thuds. The warehouse looked deserted, with broken windows high up on the graffiti-covered walls. Around the outside, scrubby bushes grew amongst knee-high grass.

"Summer, stay with me," Dillon ordered. His expression told her he expected her to follow instructions to the letter. She jerked her head in compliance. At least he hadn't suggested she wait in the car.

"She should wait in the car," Josh said.

"No." Dillon gave her a hard look. "She'll worry. Summer's better off with one of us."

"Family conference over?" Louie demanded. When Dillon gave a curt nod, he said, "Jake and I will go right. You and Josh go left." Nikolai's two friends slithered along the side of the warehouse and disappeared around the corner with the stealth of a pair of cats.

A white car pulled up farther down the street, followed by a police car.

"Do we wait for them?" Summer whispered.

"Nah," Josh said. "Let's go."

"Where are the doors? How do we get in?"

"Summer, shut up." Dillon squeezed her shoulder in silent comfort. "Don't worry. We'll find him."

Summer followed, right on Dillon's heels. They skirted the long grass and discarded litter, running low and keeping close to the rundown building.

"Keep up, Summer. Don't fall behind."

She grimaced at Dillon's broad back. Fine for him to say when he had long, ground-eating legs. She hastened her pace, breaking out into a trot. Her foot hit a hole and her ankle rolled.

"Shit."

Up ahead, Dillon and Josh froze. As one, they turned to her with their warrior faces in neutral. It took them a split second to analyze the situation, then their expressions turned from neutral to brotherly disgust.

Josh rolled his eyes and whispered in a low voice she had to strain to hear. "I don't know why we didn't stroll up to the front door and knock. We might as well—considering the noise you're making."

"You're as bad as Nikolai," she snapped.

"Keep it down," Dillon murmured, his

eyes assessing the area ahead and behind.

"Well, if you'd let me in on your little games and gave me some practice, I wouldn't blunder around like an elephant in ballet shoes. And thank you for asking, my ankle is fine."

Josh grinned. "Sis, you do have a way with words."

"If you two are finished, we need to move. Before the cops get here."

Josh and Summer sobered and fell in behind Dillon. When they reached the next corner of the warehouse, Dillon slowed and cautiously checked round the corner.

"Clear. Summer, watch where you put your feet, and if there's any gunfire, drop to the ground and crawl back in the direction we've come."

Mention of guns brought home the

reality. Dare and his men meant business. They were all in danger. Tension tightened her belly in a vice-like grip.

They crept around the corner. At the far end of the warehouse, figures appeared. She froze until she identified them. Jake and Louie.

Jake signaled with his hands. A foreign language to her, but Josh and Dillon seemed to understand.

As one, they moved along the rear of the warehouse to the open door.

Silly of them to leave the small, rear door open, Summer thought as Louie peered inside. Perhaps they felt safe because the huge roller door at the front of the warehouse was secured.

Louie signaled, then moved back. He did another series of hand signals to Josh and Dillon.

Summer tugged on Josh's arm and stood on tiptoes to whisper in his ear. "What's going on?"

"Tarei knows we're here. He's going to distract them."

Summer's stomach hollowed out again. The perfect way to lose weight—live your life in fear. "How?"

Josh shook his head and squeezed her upper arm in silent encouragement.

Summer heard a loud crash inside the warehouse. It reverberated through her body, pushing fear along every nerve ending.

"Stay here," Dillon ordered.

Summer opened her mouth to argue.

Jake stopped her with a look. "Nikolai will worry. He needs to concentrate."

Summer's breath eased out and she nodded, albeit unwillingly. "I'll wait right here."

"Stay flat against the wall." Jake's face held approval.

Another crash sounded, followed by cursing. Her brothers and Nikolai's friends slipped through the door.

For a few moments, she stayed against the wall just as they'd told her, but the crashes and thumps coming from inside the warehouse became louder. She crept to the door and peered inside. A hand snapped out and grabbed her shirt.

"Knew you couldn't resist poking your nose in," a familiar voice growled.

"Nikolai!" Summer flew through the door into his arms and hugged him tight. Then she stood at arm's length to survey the damage. She made a tsking sound and traced the swollen area around his cheekbone. "You're going to have a black eye."

"Yeah." Nikolai grabbed her and hugged her tight as though he couldn't believe she was safe. He buried his face in her hair, and his chest rose and fell.

"Hands up. Against the wall." The harsh voice grabbed their unwilling attention.

"It's the cops," Nikolai murmured against her ear. "Follow their instructions. They're not sure who the bad guys are yet."

Summer glanced toward the door. The rigid stance of the cop in the doorway backed up his words. She raised her hands as did Nikolai. His brown eyes bore silent encouragement and a trace of concern.

"I'm fine," she whispered. "Whupped Dare's hide and kicked him in the balls."

Nikolai's bark of laughter drew a frown from the cop who'd issued the instructions. "You two. Shut it."

Behind them, her brothers, Jake and Louie had overpowered Dare's cohorts. All four men stood to attention, their warrior's faces in evidence. Nikolai had his warrior's face on too. Summer stared at him, unable to look away. Dangerous. Hard. Then one brown eye closed in a wink. It was so uncharacteristic her mouth gaped in astonishment.

Nikolai glanced at the cops then moved his hand from the wall. He traced the outline of her smiling mouth, his eyes dark and intent. Her pulse skipped in an excited blip.

The cops entered the room cautiously—six of them—and fanned out. The last one through the door jerked his head at Jake in a gesture of greeting.

"Bro. You've done our work for us." His wide grin told Summer his temperament was similar to Jake's—easygoing and fun.

"'Bout time you guys got here. Hey, lovebirds. Cut that out," Jake drawled.

Summer jerked her gaze from Nikolai's, and tried to control the burst of heat to her cheeks as she glanced around the cavernous warehouse.

Two of Dare's gang lay on the floor, looking worse for wear. One groaned and attempted to crawl away until a policeman fastened handcuffs around his wrists and stood him up. The third man leaned against a wooden packing case, blood dripping from his face onto the concrete floor.

Jake and his brother went into a huddle. Jake nodded and the pair walked over to her and Nikolai.

"Thanks to your information we've stopped a large shipment of new designer drugs coming into the country. The customs agents didn't spot them because Dare and overseas partners have developed a way of affixing the drugs to the back of stickers. Owner of the super yacht said he designed kids' sticker books and had boxes of samples on board. No one thought anything of it until we intercepted the message and looked closer."

"Wow," Summer said. "But who planted the drugs in Uncle Henry's house? And ran me off the road? I don't think that was Dare. He wouldn't have wanted to point our minds in the direction of drugs. And when he found out, he acted strange."

"Martin is in a territory struggle with the Ngataki family. We think Josiah Ngataki was trying to make trouble for Martin, and Ngataki thought you were important to him. You got caught in the middle," Jake's brother said.

"He mentioned someone called Ngataki."

Nikolai curled his arm around her waist. "Can we go?"

"We need them for questioning," one of the cops said.

Her brother, Dillon, interceded. "Can you question them tomorrow? They've been through a fair bit today. We can answer most of your immediate questions. If they promise to drop into the Auckland Central station tomorrow, could you let them go home?"

"Dillon," Josh muttered, a look of amazement on his face. "I thought we'd agreed."

"I've changed my mind. Summer is old enough to make her own decisions. We got into the habit of watching out for her when she was sick as a kid. It's time we stopped."

Josh's brows drew together. His head shook as he looked from her to Nikolai. "I don't think Mum—"

"We're not telling Mum," Dillon said.

"No, I am," Summer said.

While she dreaded telling her parents, particularly her mother, that she intended to stay in Auckland, adults took responsibility. If she balked at telling her parents about Nikolai, then what hope was there for their future?

Chapter 19

"Will you marry me?"

Summer's blunt question echoed in the huge warehouse. The cops discussing whether they could go without giving a statement stopped talking to stare.

Jake tipped him a wink. Louie chuckled while Summer's brothers started to rumble like waking volcanoes.

Nikolai swallowed. It did nothing to disperse the lump of tension lodged in his throat. He ran his hand across her cheek and tucked a blue strand of hair behind her ear, the familiar action relaxing him. "Are you pregnant?"

The rumbling from her brothers grew louder, but he ignored them to focus on

Summer.

His lover. And now—his wife-to-be.

A month ago, the thought would have scared him spitless. But today a surge of anticipation throbbed through him.

"Well?" Dillon demanded. "Are you pregnant?" His disapproval bled into his expression, making him appear tough and mean.

"None of your business," she inserted smoothly into the pulsing silence left while her brother scowled at Nikolai. "In other words, butt out."

A laugh sounded from one of the policemen, abruptly cut off when Dillon's attention focused on him.

Nikolai decided it was time to take control. He cupped her elbow and exerted a little force. No way was he baring his heart in public. Their sex life had received enough discussion already.

Now was the time for privacy.

"We'll see you tomorrow," he said to Jake's brother. "Around ten?" After receiving a nod of approval, he urged Summer out the door, despite the glares from her brothers and the shooting pain from his knee. Summer didn't need to know that Dare's goons had done a good job on roughing him up.

"Good exit." Humor lurked in her beautiful blue eyes, and Nikolai forgot the jagged pain. "But how are we going to get home? We don't have a car."

His gaze roved her face. Her blue eyes sparkled with life and humor. Her pink lips curved in a secret smile. A jolt of pure lust laced with possessiveness raced through his body, stirring his cock to life. She didn't look like a woman who had to get married. Confidence and assurance blazed from her. She looked like a woman with sex on her mind.

"Wait there, and I'll grab Louie's keys. They can call a cab. Then we need to talk."

"Are you sure you're all right?" Summer said when he returned.

"Don't you want to marry an old crock like me? You gonna change your mind?"

She halted beside Louie's car. "Not only am I not going to change my mind about marrying you, I want to have your children too." A challenging glint glowed in her blue eyes.

Nikolai stared, mesmerized by her beauty. His woman. He ran his fingers down her silky cheek, trying to ignore the throbbing bumps and bruises on his ribs, inflicted by the clotheshorse's thugs. "As long as you agree to marry me, you can have anything you want."

"But not straightaway, please. I want to

have you to myself for a few years."

Nikolai grinned suddenly. "Not finished with your research yet?"

"That's right." She gave an enthusiastic nod. "I found this neat book in the secondhand bookshop. A bit racy for the library," she added.

"I love you."

"I know," Summer said in a smug tone. "I finally worked it out. The feeling is mutual." She paused, her forehead puckering into a cute frown. "Except when you try to boss me around. I don't like orders. I like—"

"To be asked," Nikolai finished.

Okay. He could learn to live with her independent streak. It looked as though this babysitting assignment was turning into a permanent one. Who'd have thought? But the idea of waking up each morning beside Summer didn't scare him. He smirked as he pressed a kiss to her mouth. Not too much, anyway.

"Just remember that I like to be asked for my opinion and our marriage will be a big success." Summer reinforced the sentiment. As the sound of voices grew louder, she glanced toward the rear of the warehouse and back at him.

Nikolai moved toward the car in silent accord. "I think we should disappear before they decide to keep us here."

"You just want to have your wicked way with me."

Nikolai opened the door for her and climbed into the driver's side. "Damn straight." He leaned over to kiss her and cop a feel of her beautiful breasts at the same time.

A full-time commitment with Summer.

A wife.

His wife.

The thought should have terrified him. Knowing Summer, he'd suffer a few gray hairs in the process, but he wouldn't have it any other way.

Nikolai winked at her, a sense of rightness settling in his heart.

"Let's go then." Summer lifted her chin and stared at him in clear challenge.

"Good idea," he said, a grin of real anticipation curling across his face. He fired up the car and pulled away from the curb. "I'm ready to go home and get horizontal. We have new positions to try."

About Shelley

USA Today bestselling author Shelley Munro lives in Auckland, the City of Sails, with her husband and a cheeky Jack Russell/mystery breed dog.

Typical New Zealanders, Shelley and her husband left home for their big OE soon after they married (translation of New Zealand speak - big overseas experience). A twelve-month-long adventure lengthened to six years of roaming the world. Enduring memories include being almost sat on by a mountain gorilla in Rwanda, lazing on white sandy beaches in India, whale watching in Alaska, searching for leprechauns in Ireland, and dealing with ghosts in an English pub.

While travel is still a big attraction, these days Shelley is most likely found in front of her computer following another love - that of writing stories of contemporary and paranormal romance and adventure. Other interests include watching rugby (strictly for research purposes), cycling, playing croquet and the ukelele, and curling up with an enjoyable book.

Visit Shelley at her Website
https://shelleymunro.com

Join Shelley's Newsletter
https://shelleymunro.com/newsletter

Other Books by Shelley

Military Men

Innocent Next Door

Soldiers with Benefits

Safeguarding Sorrel

Stranded with Ella

Josh's Fake Fiancée

Operation Flower Petal

Protecting the Bride